Snow Fall

Snow Marie Reese

Snow Fall
by Snow Marie Reese

First Printing, 2015
ISBN 978-0-9862358-2-5
Twin Scale Media LLC
Colorado Springs, Co

www.twinscalemedia.com

Models:
Snow Marie Reese
Joe Rochel
Matthew Lenzi

Costumes:
Miss Melly
&
Snow Marie Reese

Snow & Red's
Hair & Makeup:
Cosmiix Artistry, makeup by Dania Blanco

Photography:
Joseph James

Story & Compositing:
Snow Marie Reese

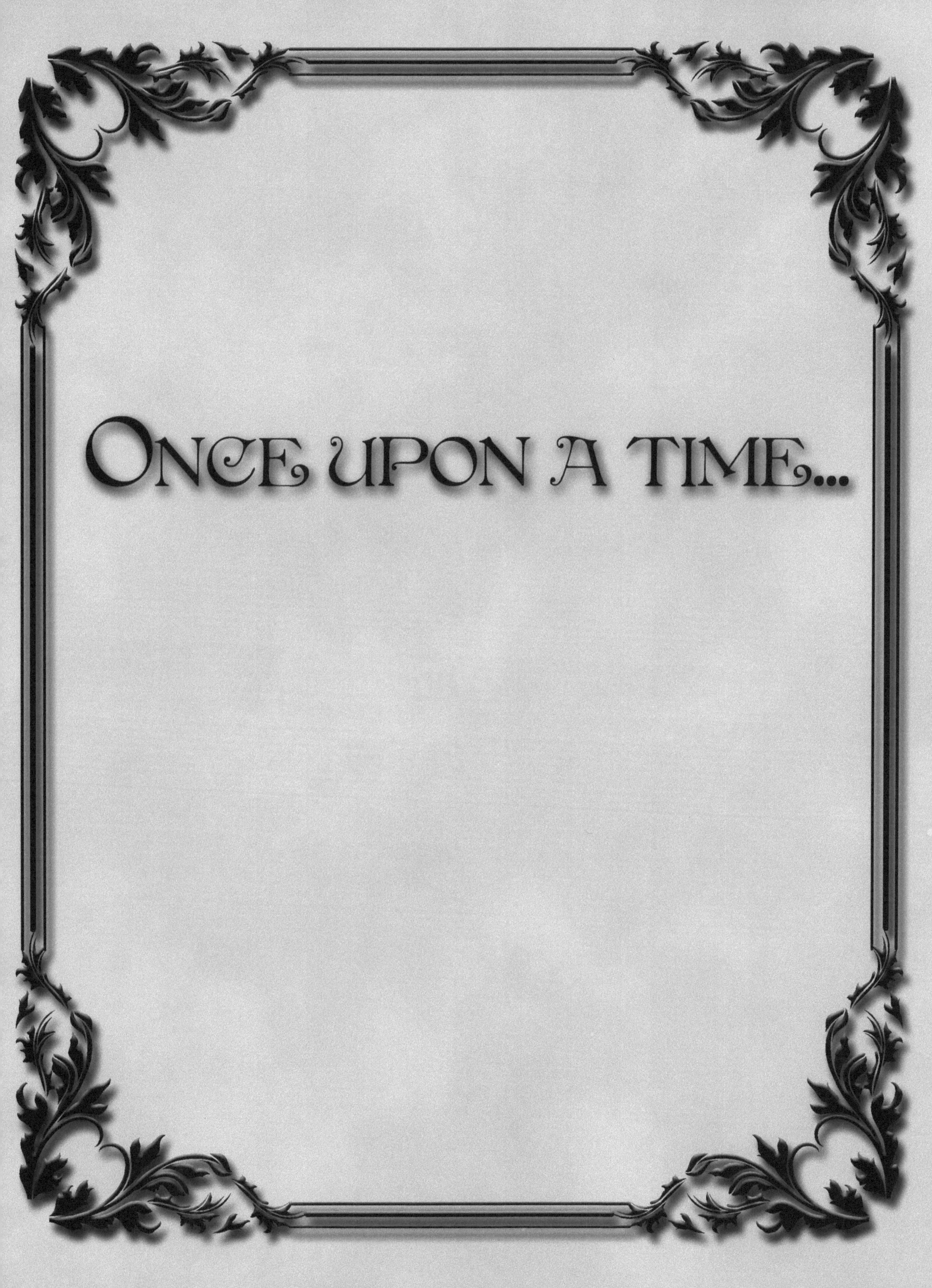
Once upon a time...

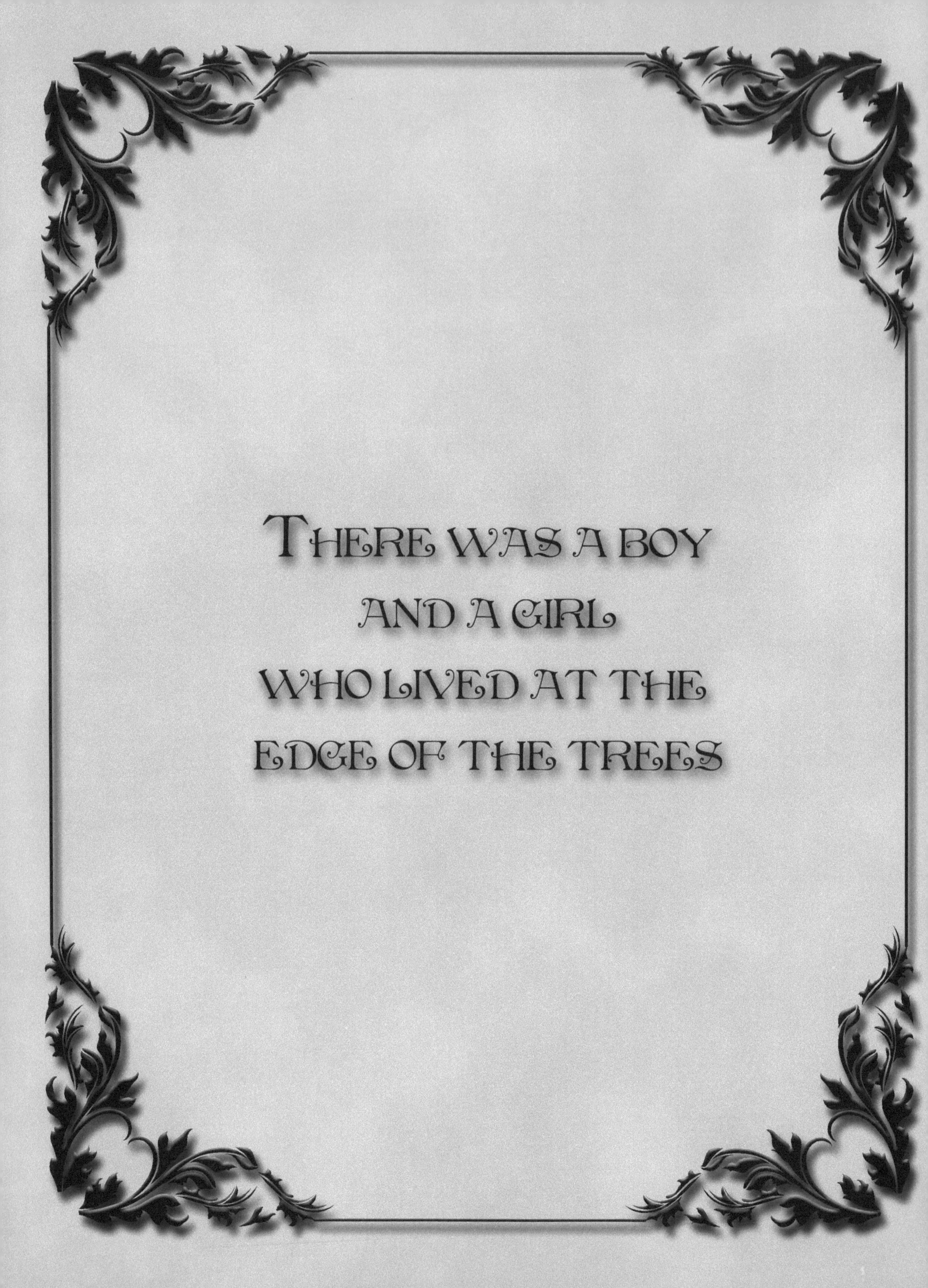

THERE WAS A BOY
AND A GIRL
WHO LIVED AT THE
EDGE OF THE TREES

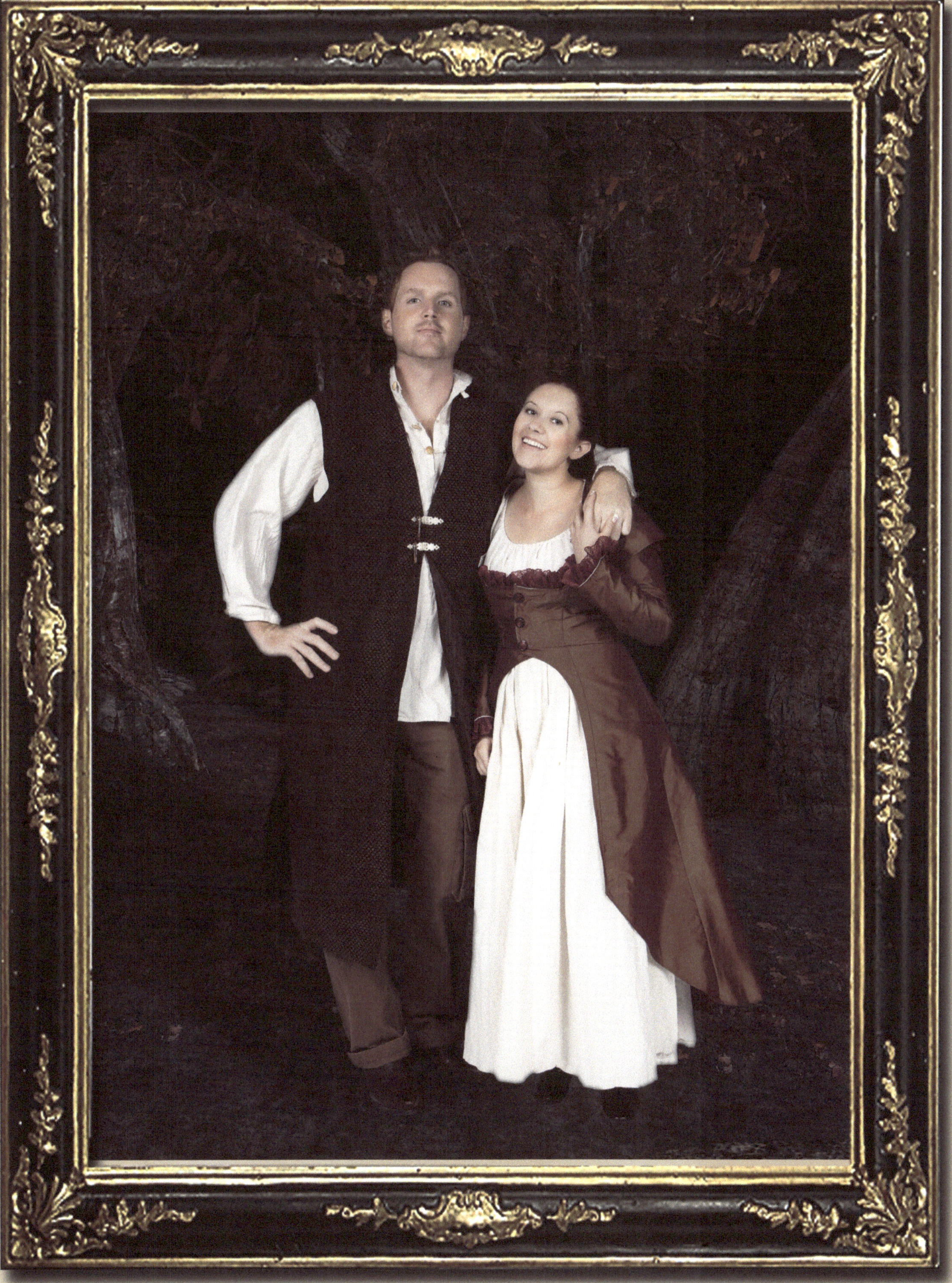

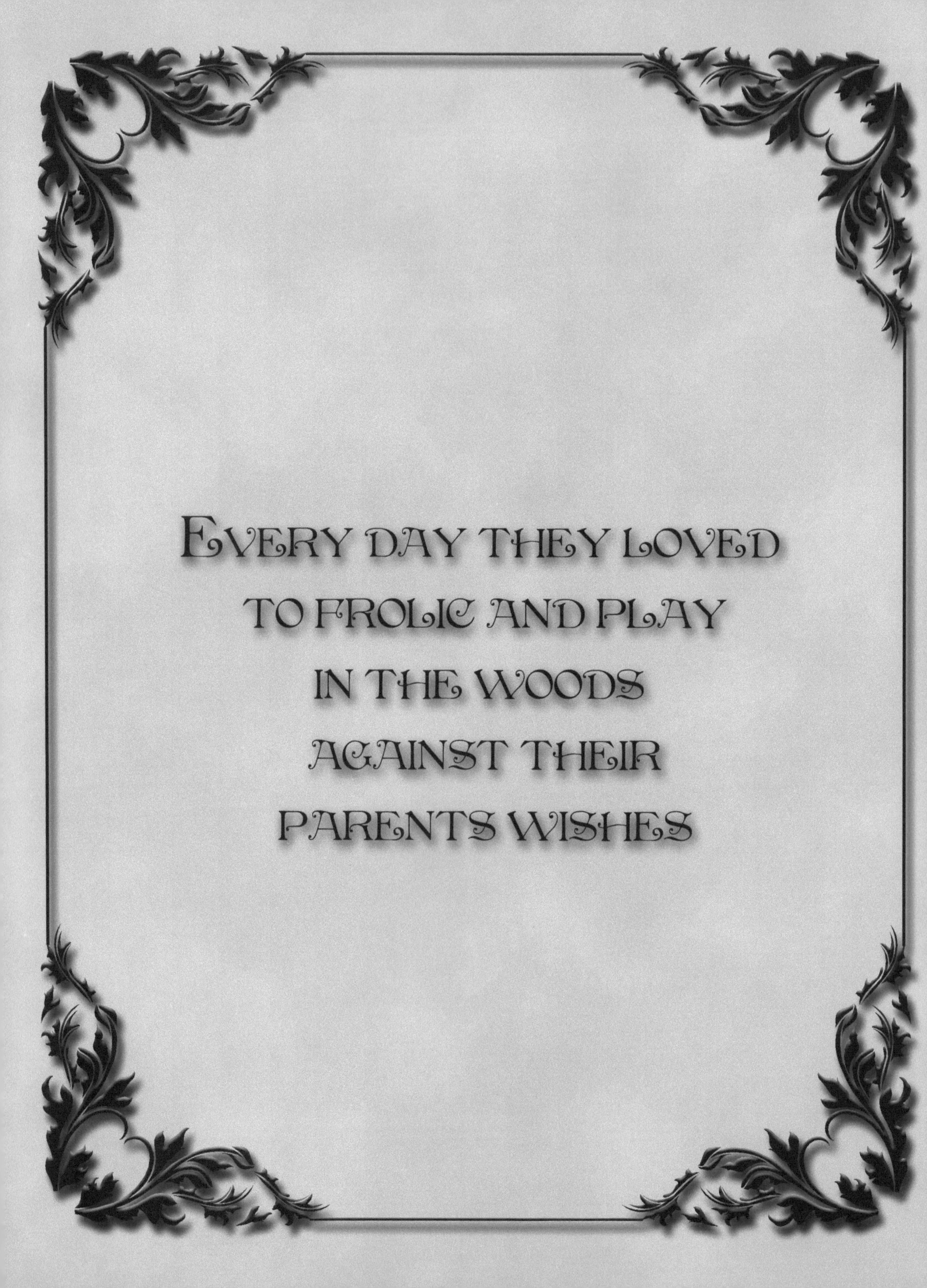

Every day they loved
to frolic and play
in the woods
against their
parents wishes

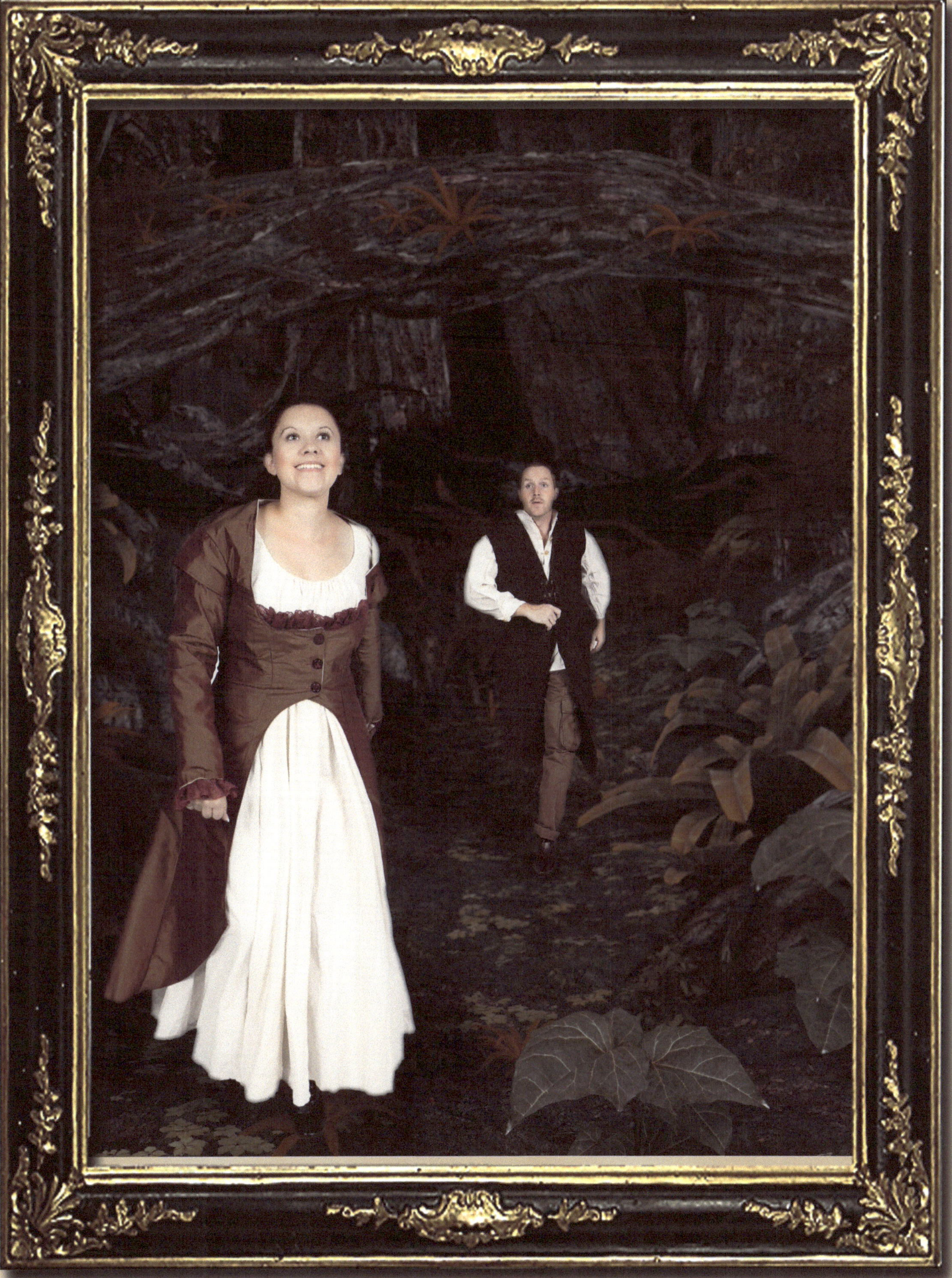

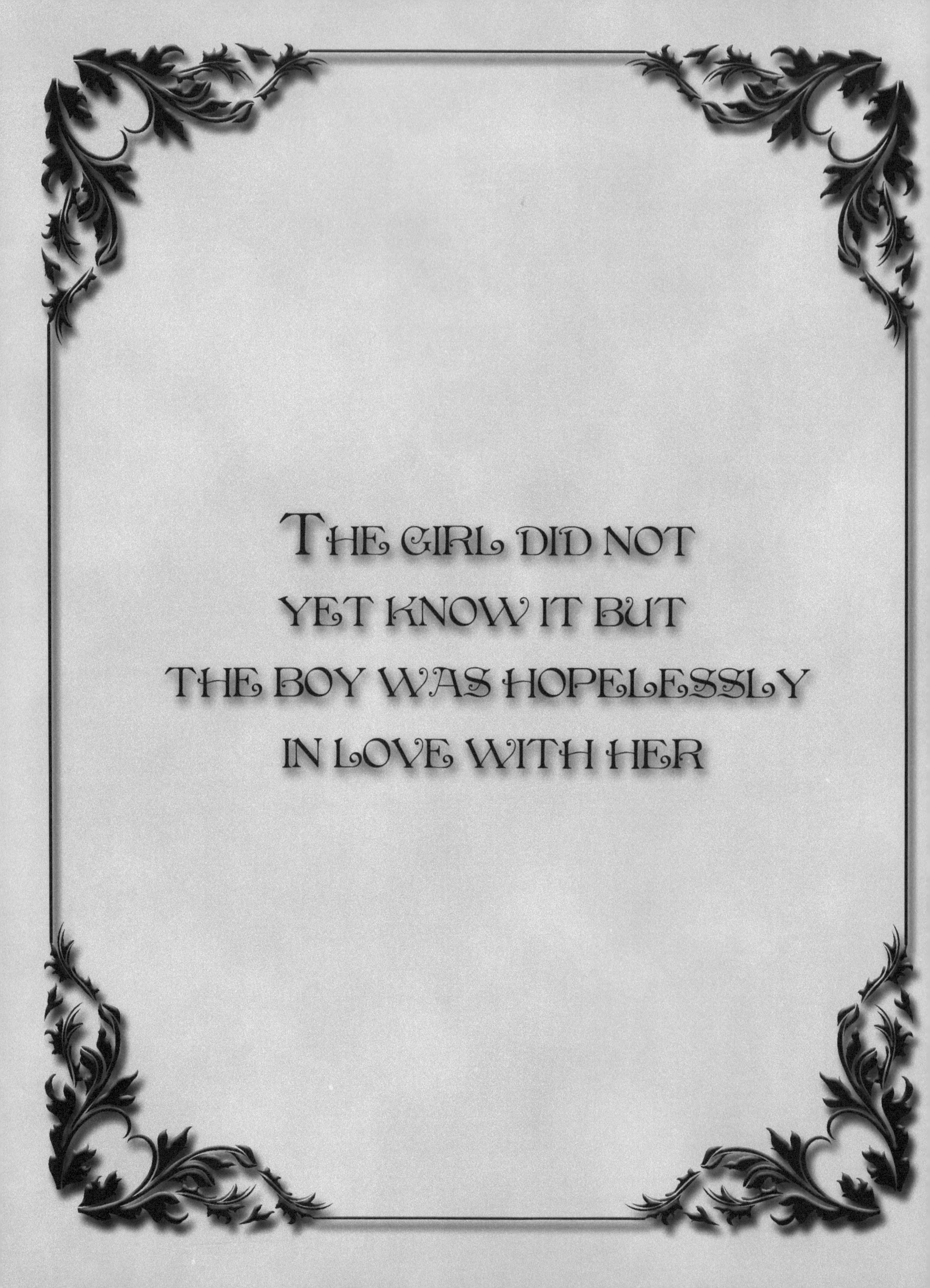

THE GIRL DID NOT
YET KNOW IT BUT
THE BOY WAS HOPELESSLY
IN LOVE WITH HER

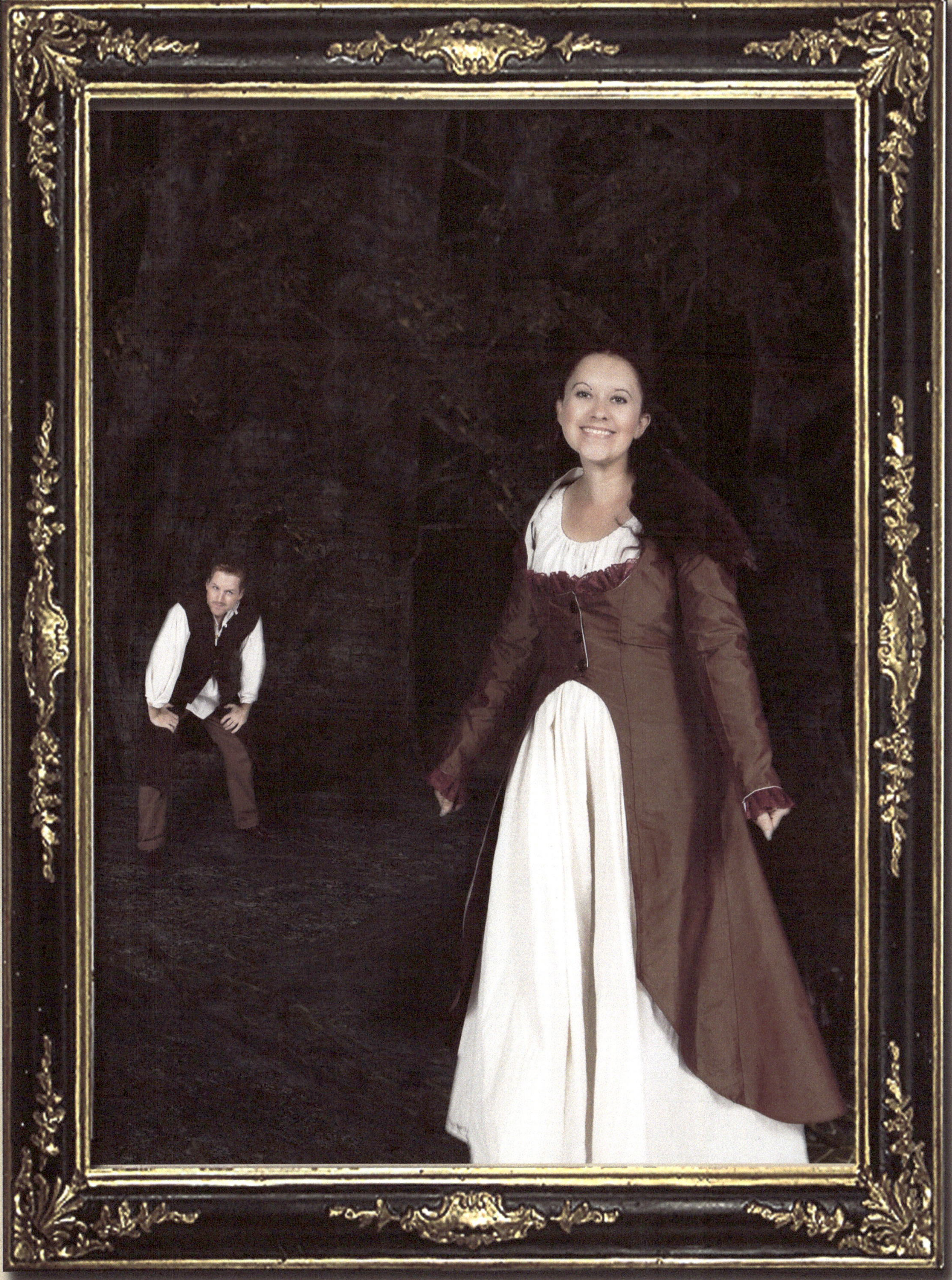

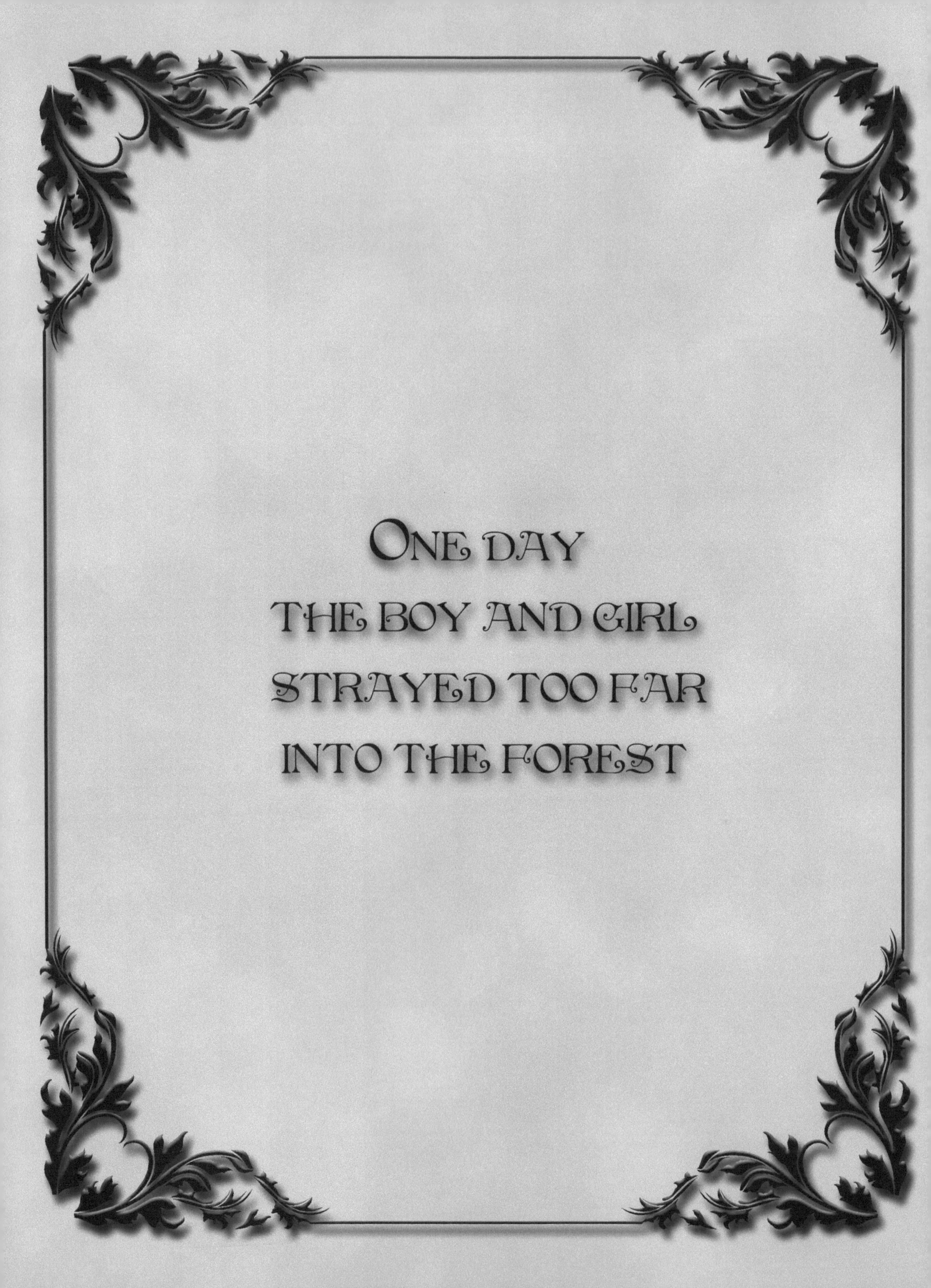
ONE DAY
THE BOY AND GIRL
STRAYED TOO FAR
INTO THE FOREST

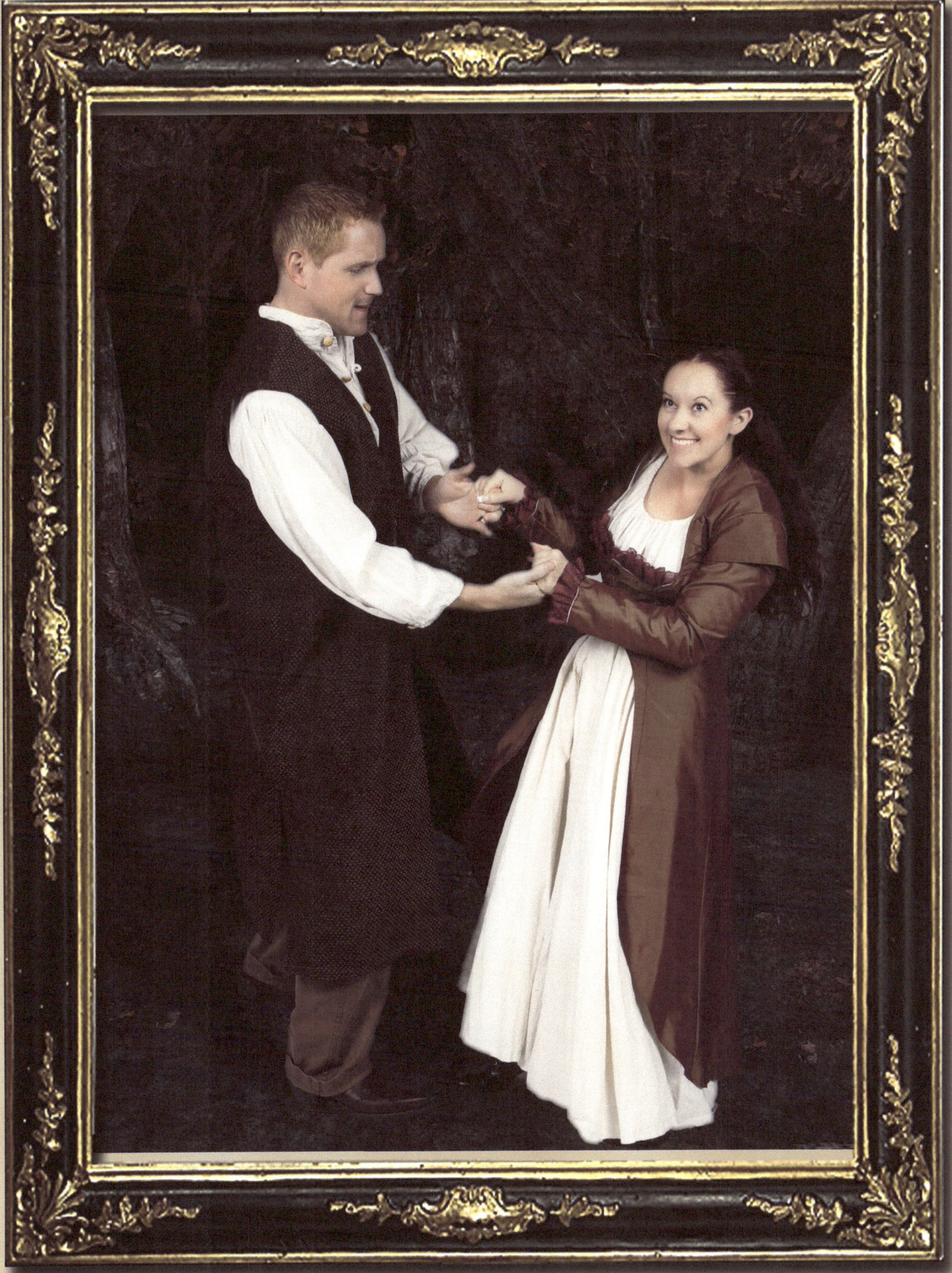

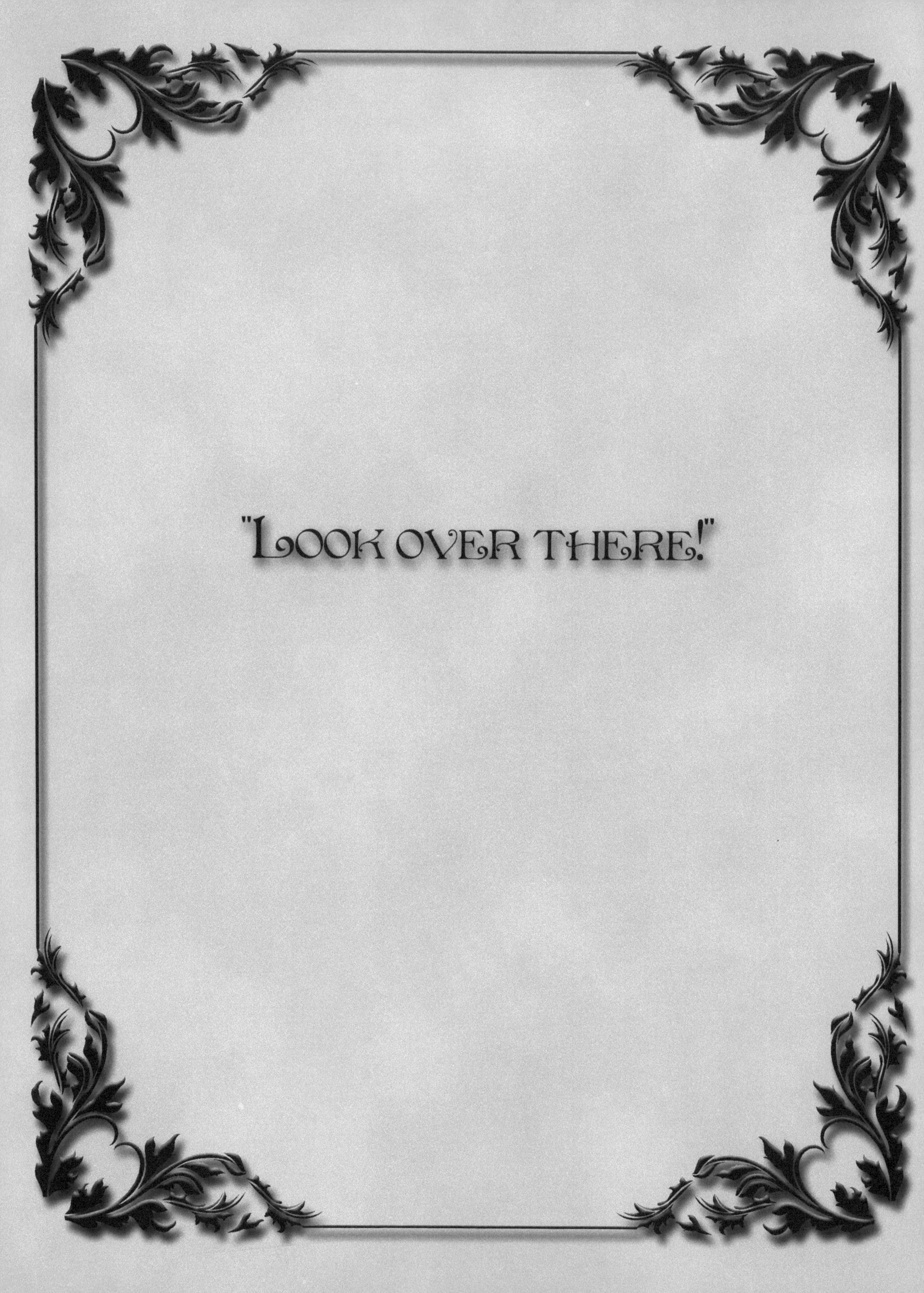
"Look over there!"

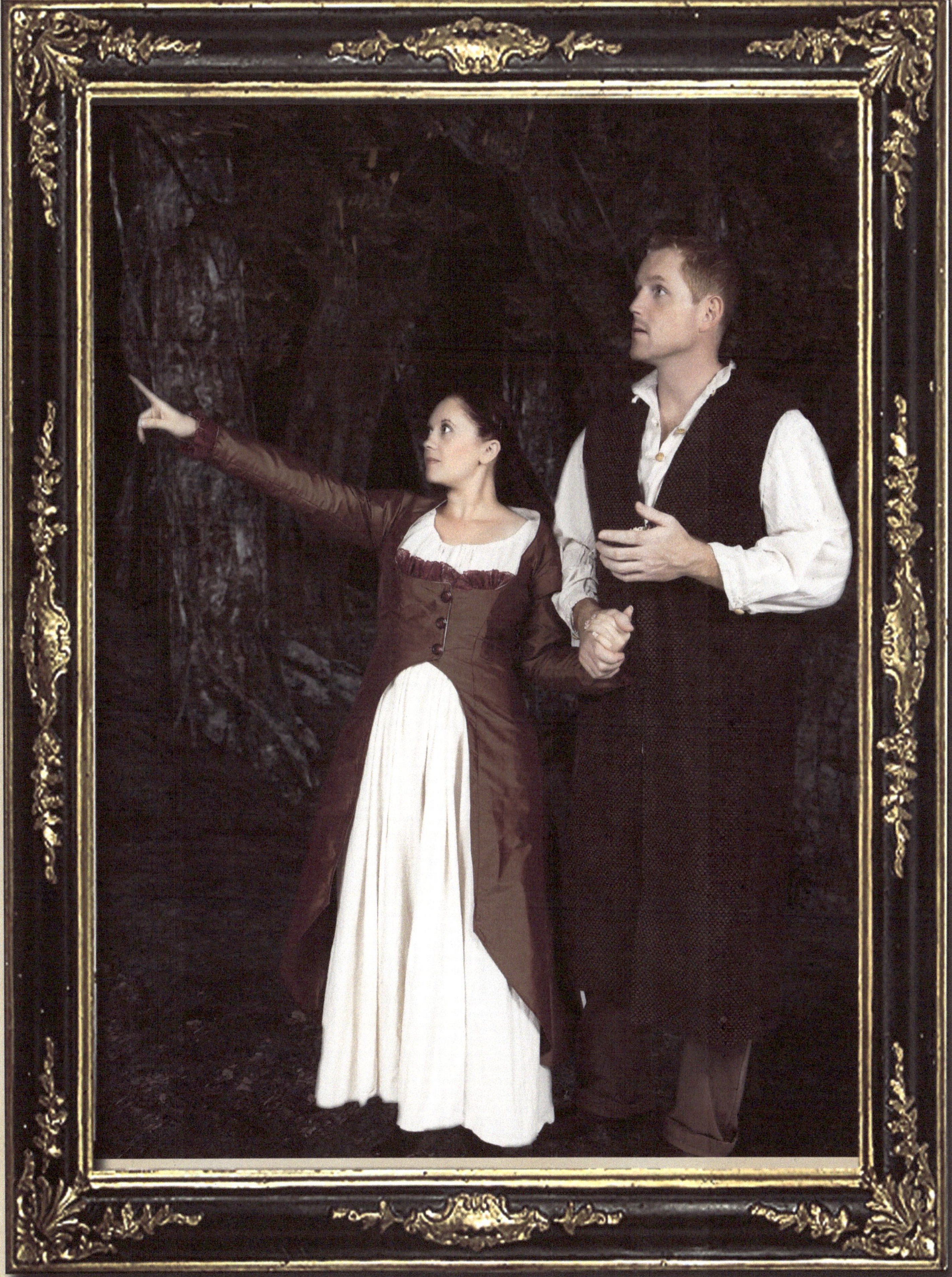

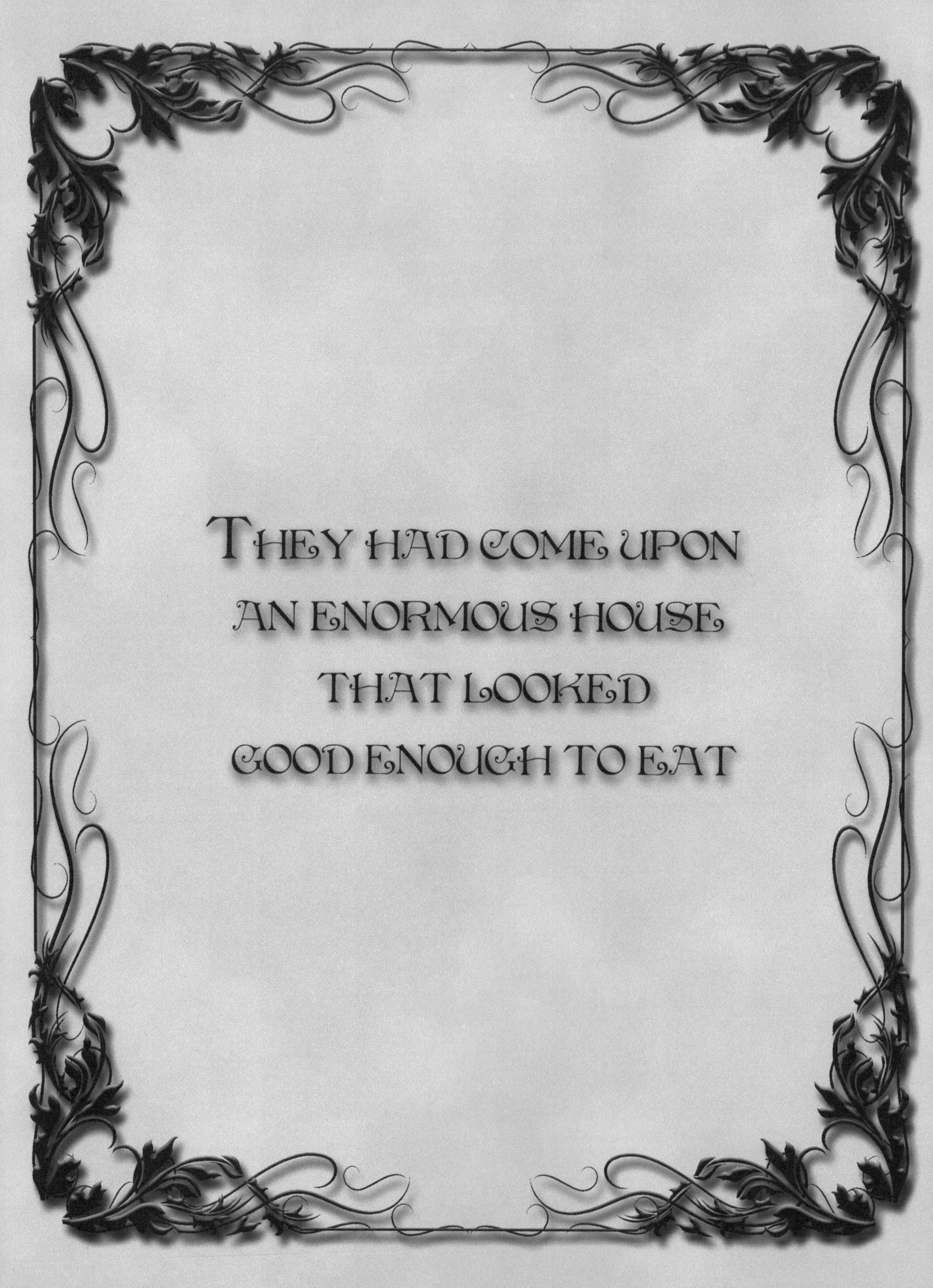
THEY HAD COME UPON
AN ENORMOUS HOUSE
THAT LOOKED
GOOD ENOUGH TO EAT

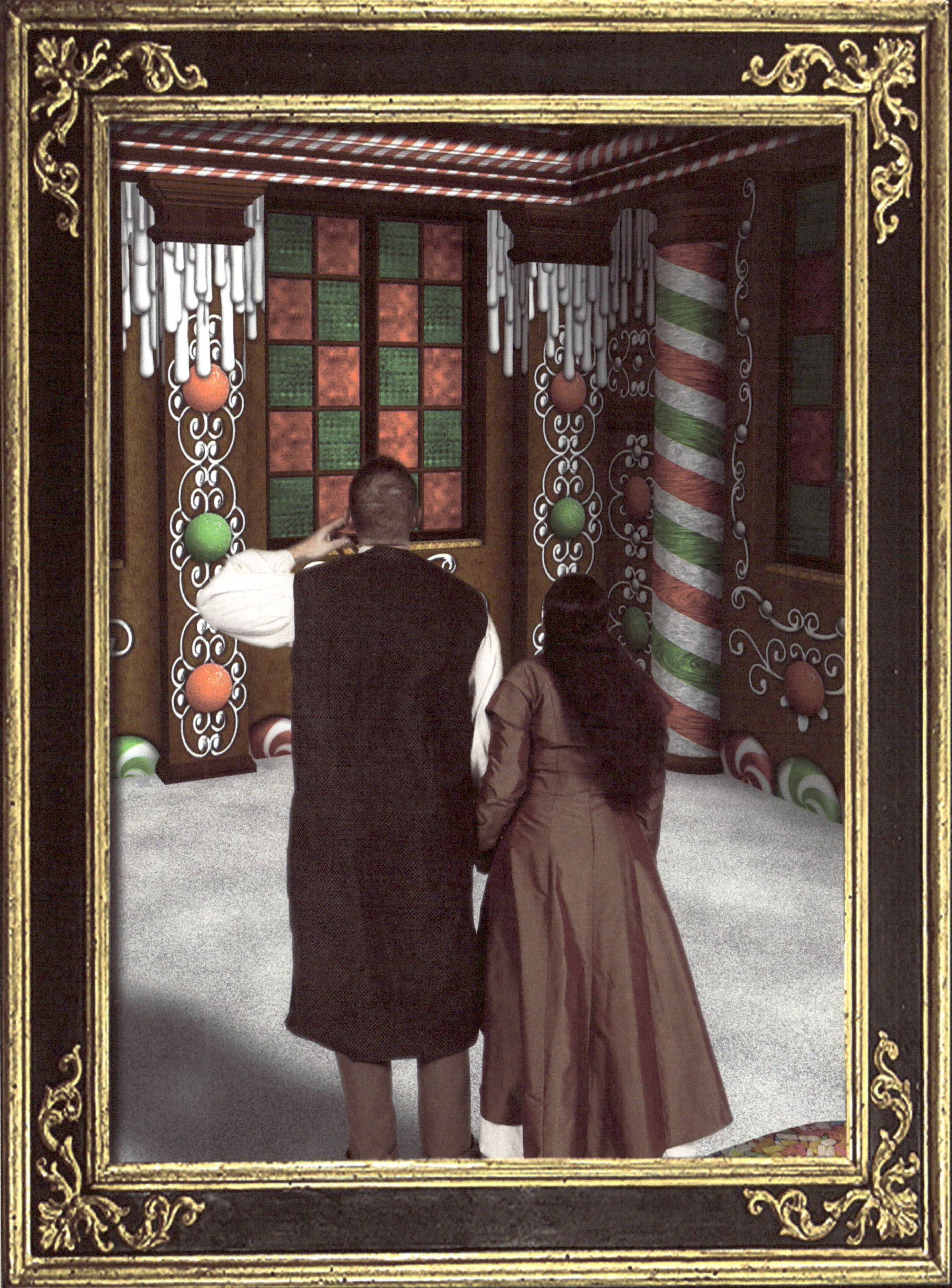

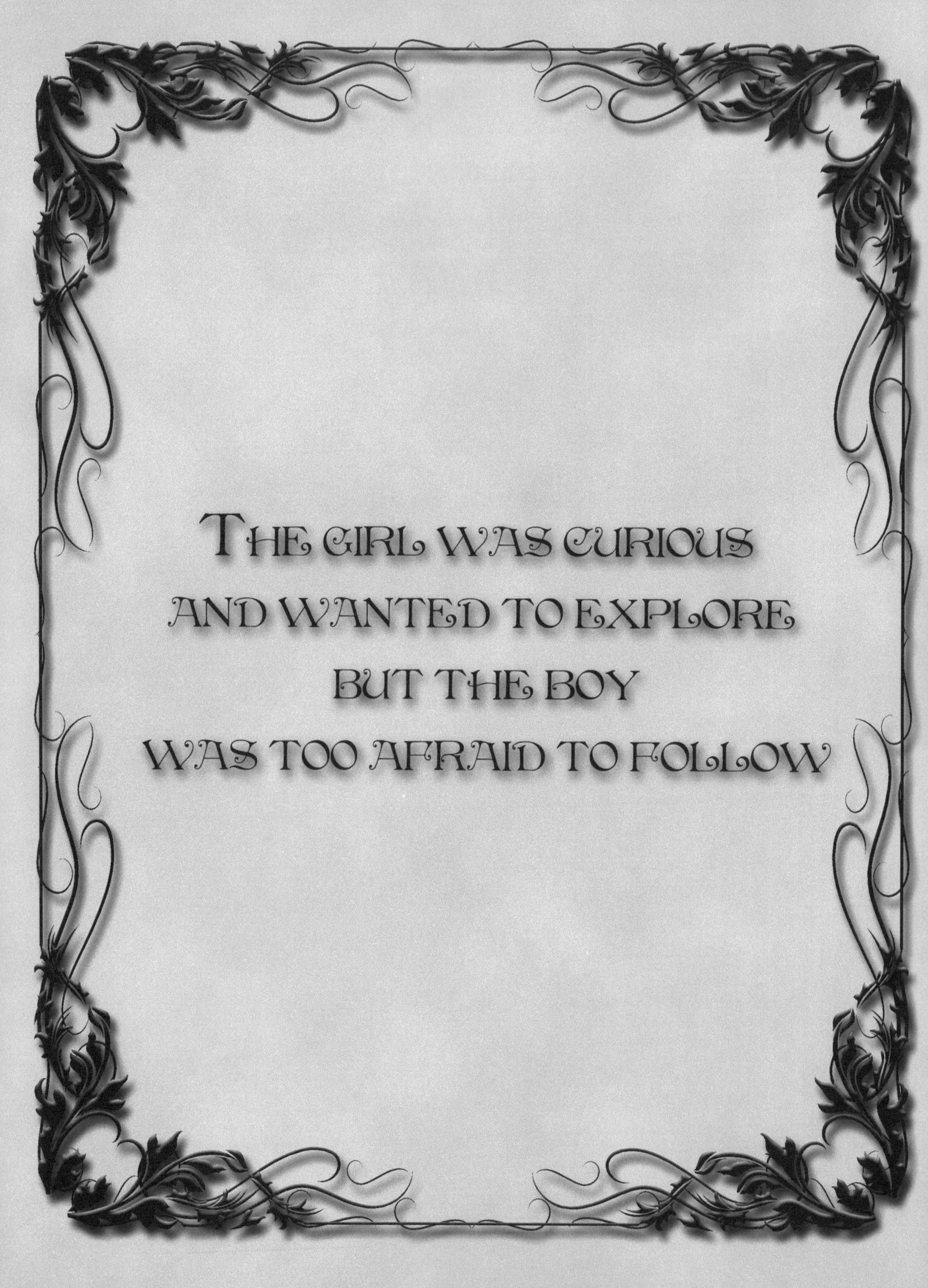
THE GIRL WAS CURIOUS
AND WANTED TO EXPLORE
BUT THE BOY
WAS TOO AFRAID TO FOLLOW

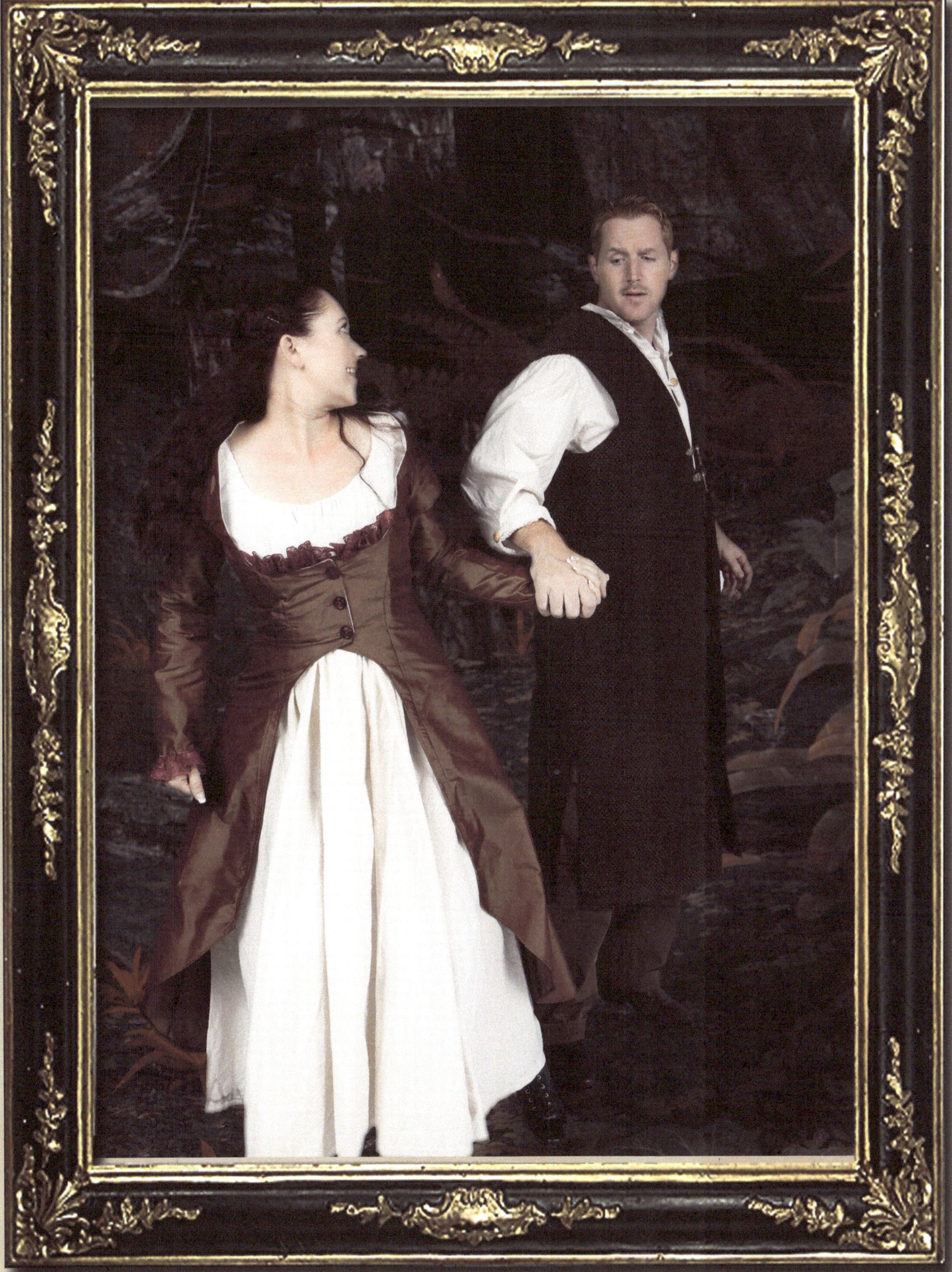

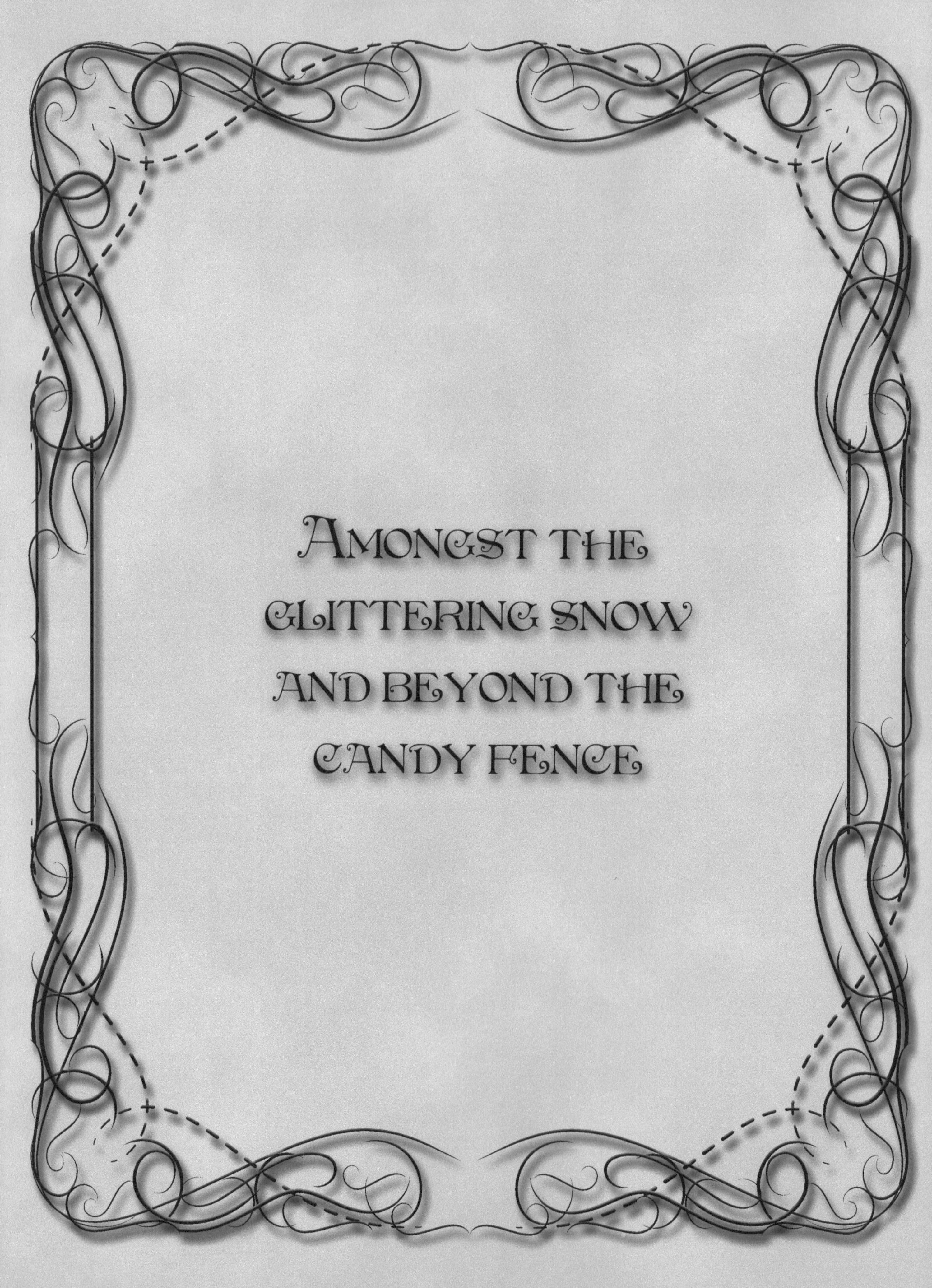

Amongst the Glittering Snow and Beyond the Candy Fence

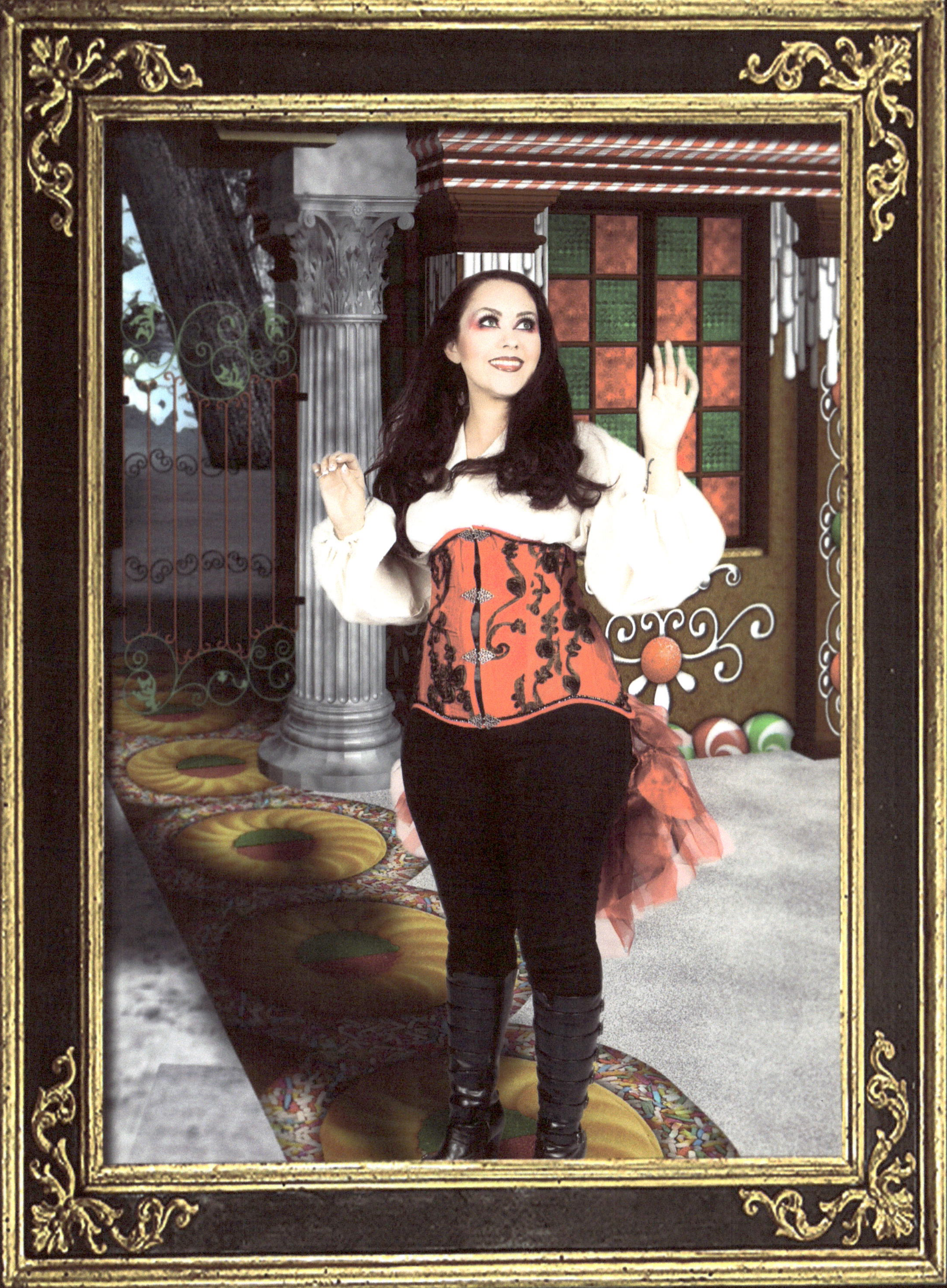

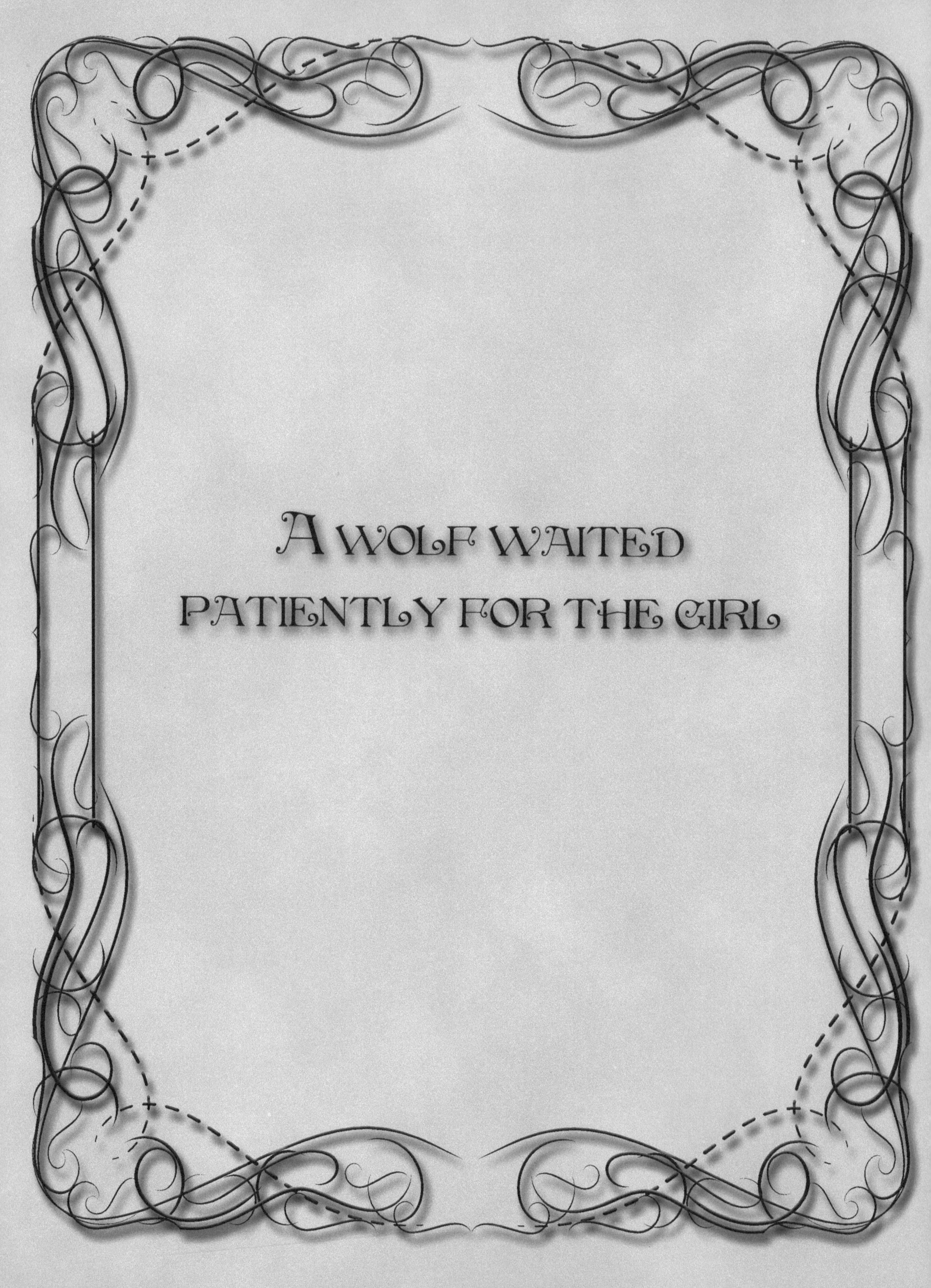
A WOLF WAITED
PATIENTLY FOR THE GIRL

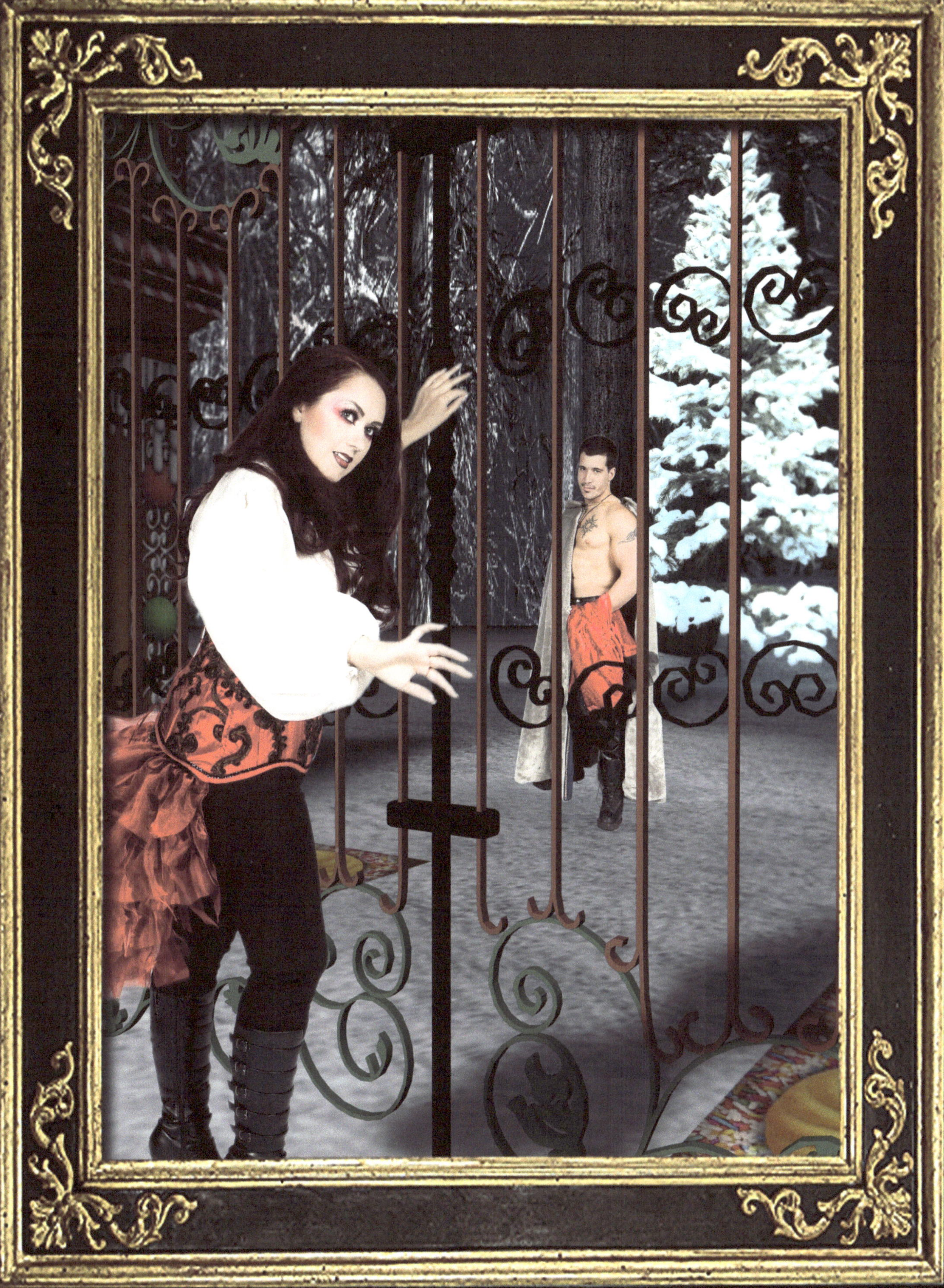

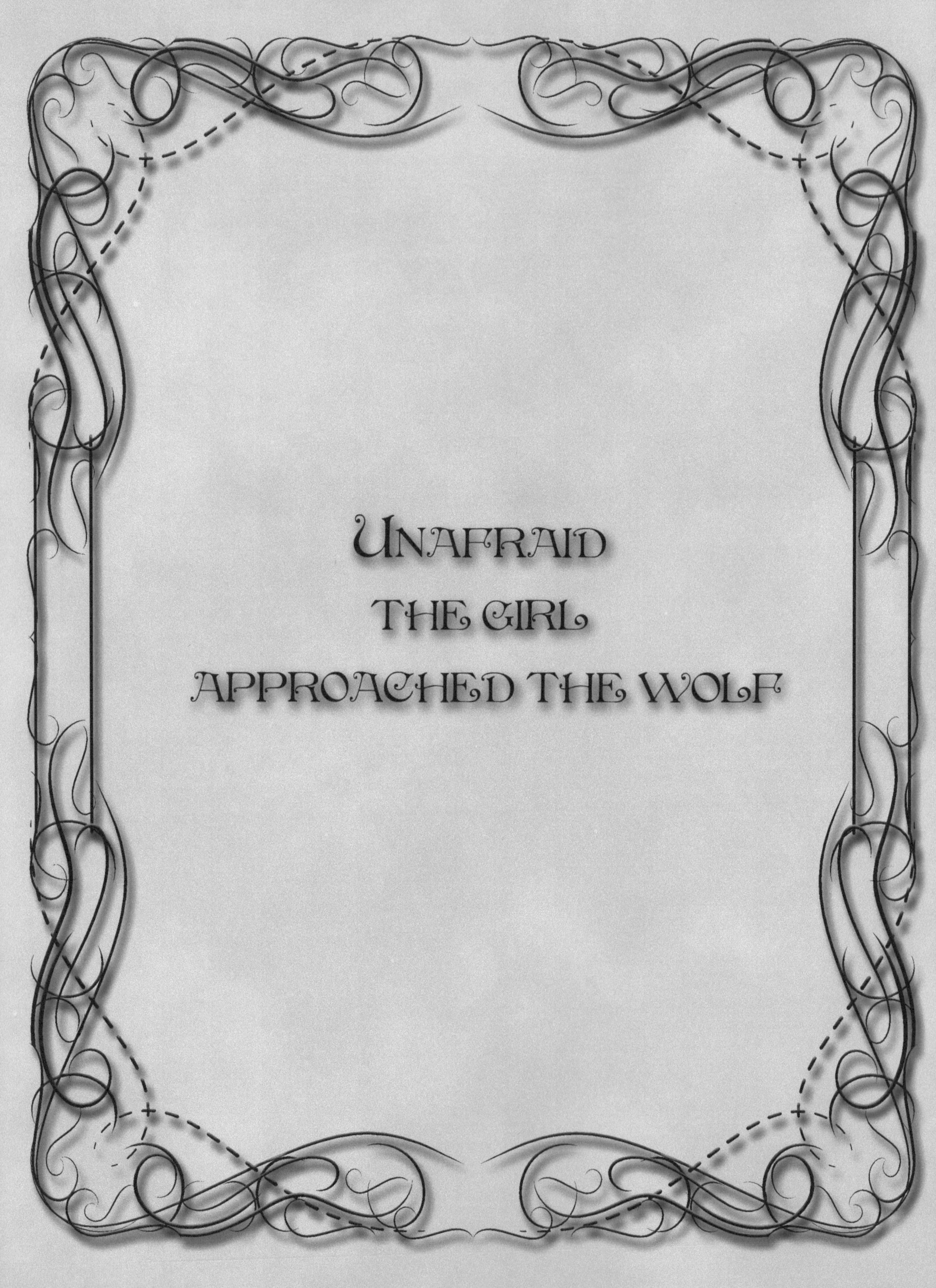

UNAFRAID
THE GIRL
APPROACHED THE WOLF

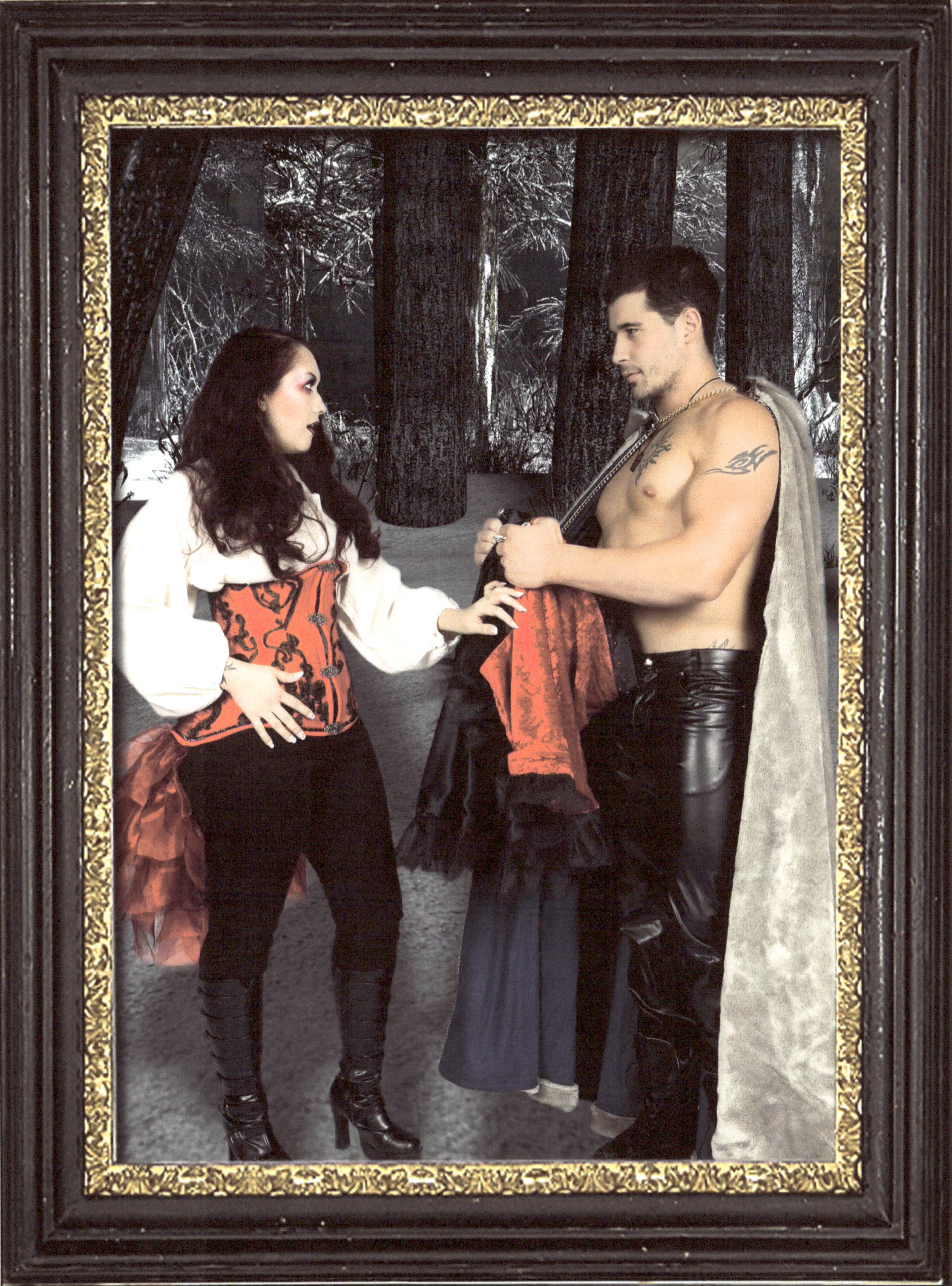

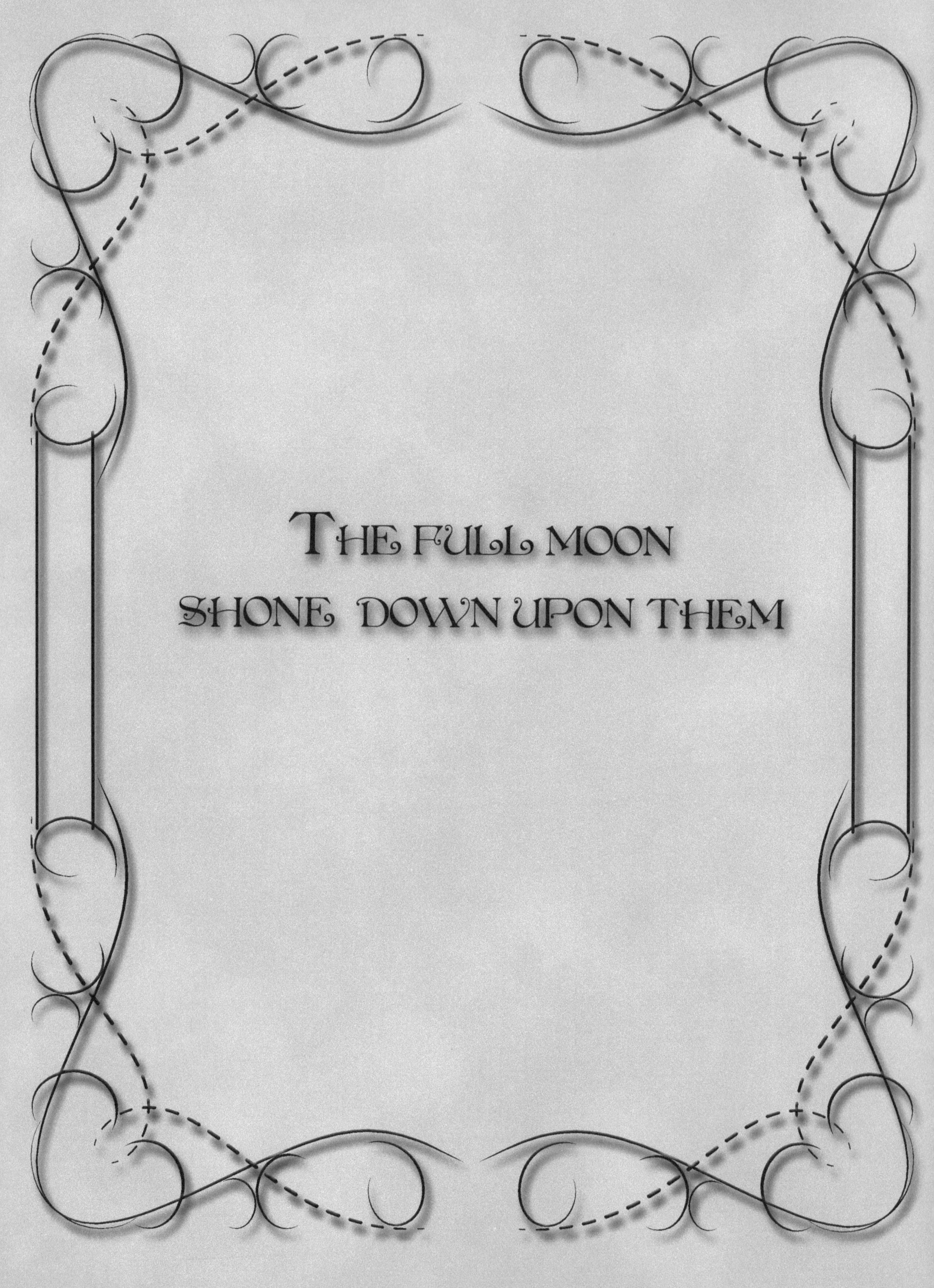
THE FULL MOON
SHONE DOWN UPON THEM

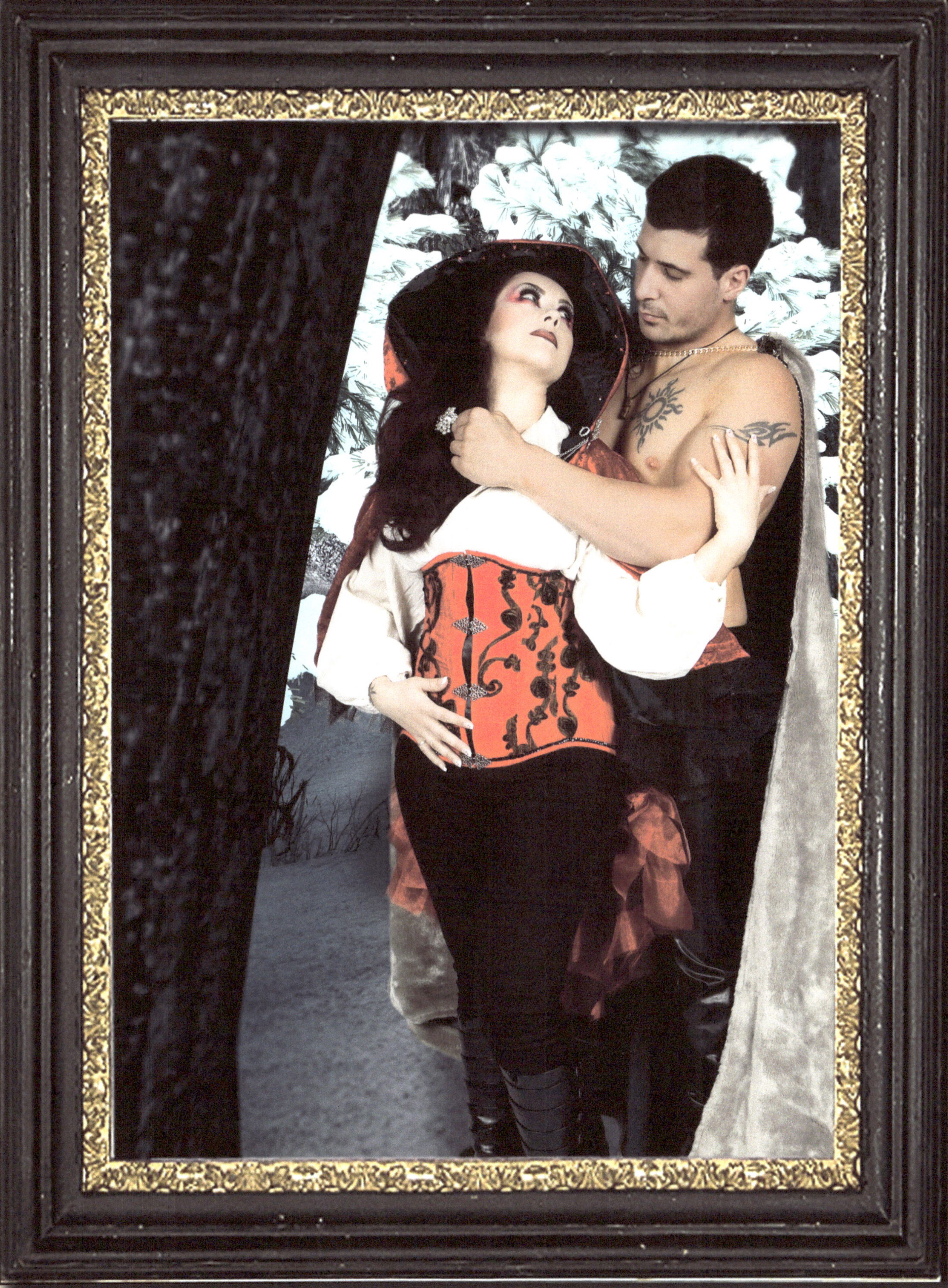

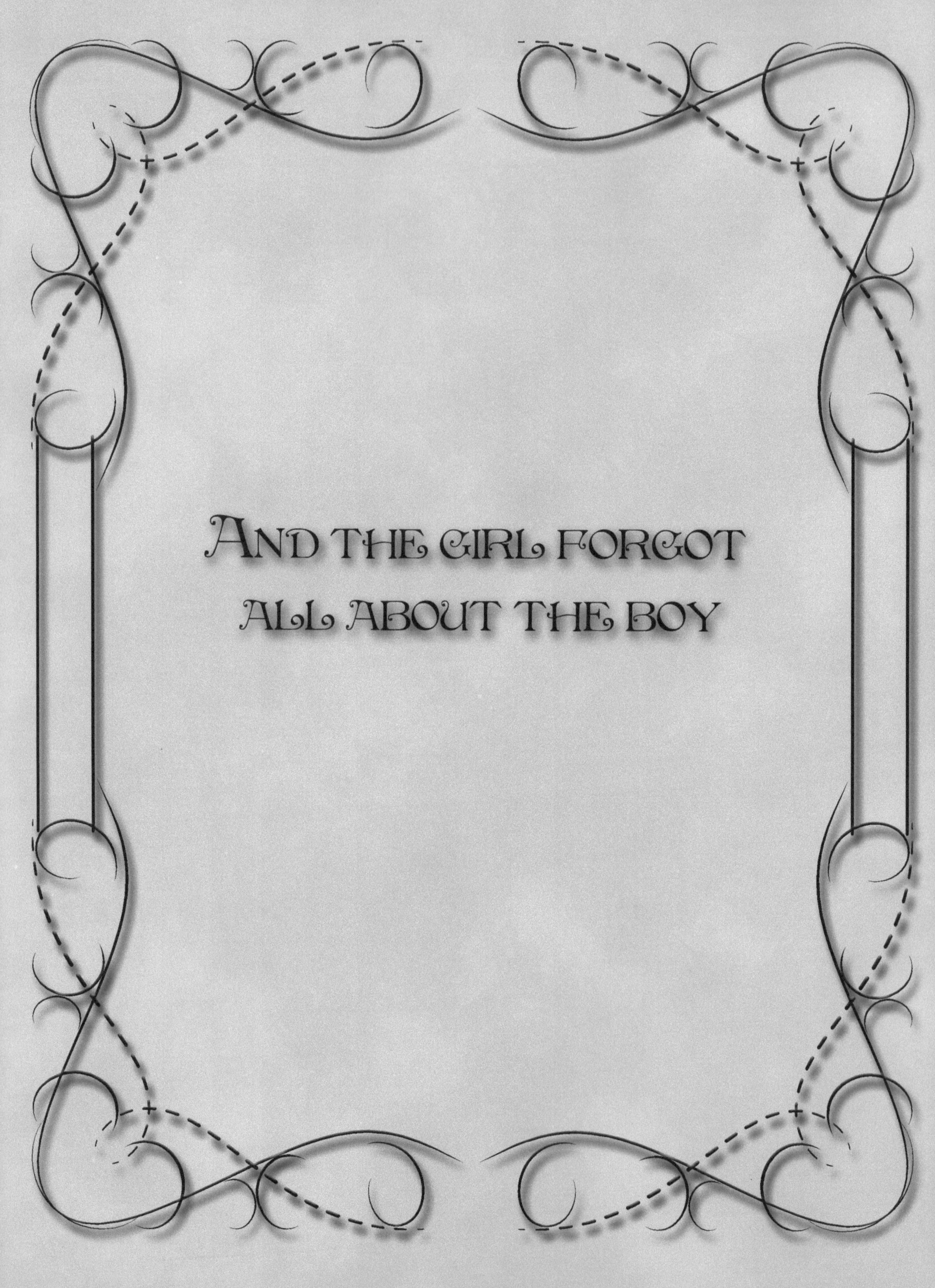
AND THE GIRL FORGOT
ALL ABOUT THE BOY

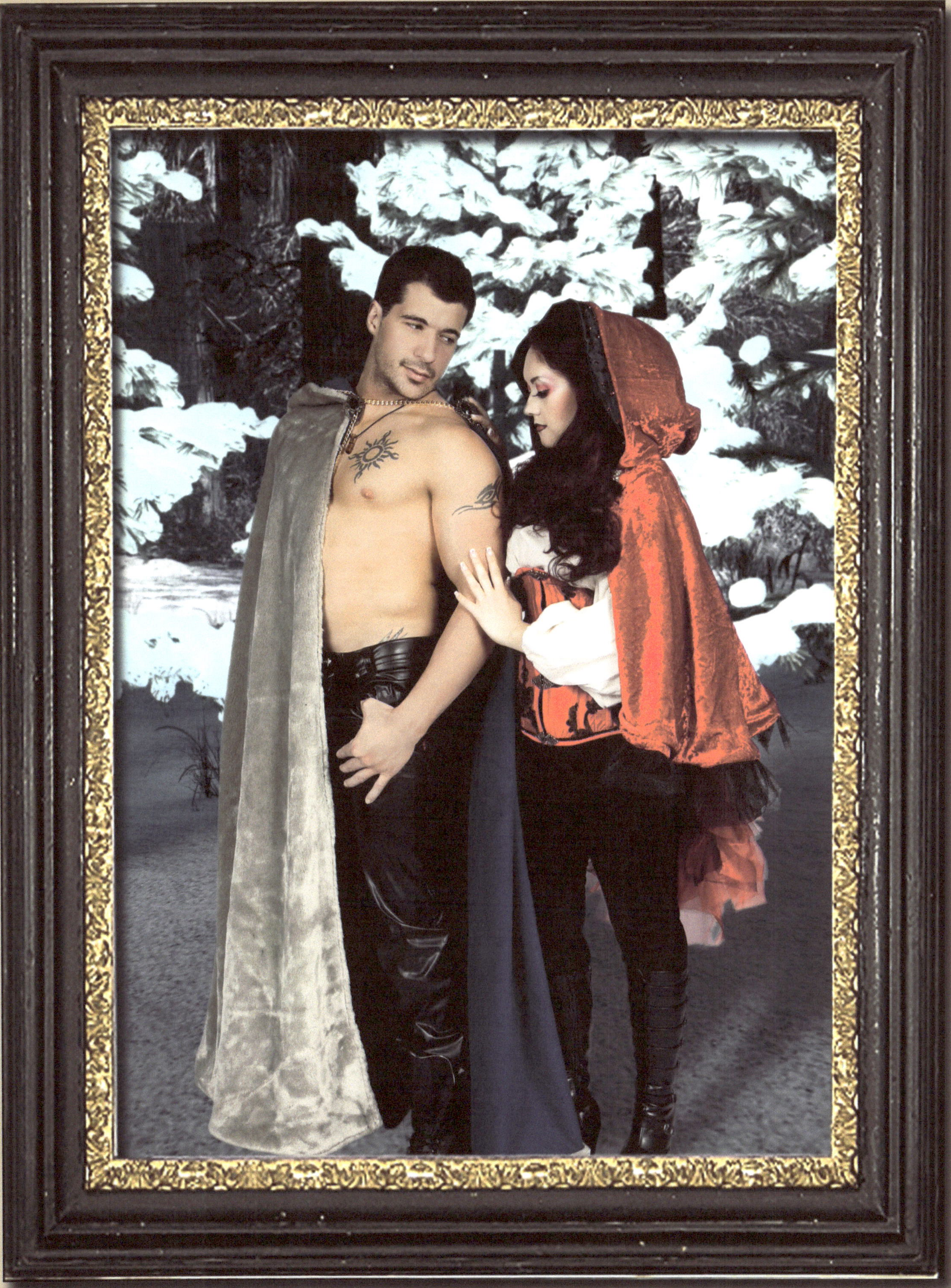

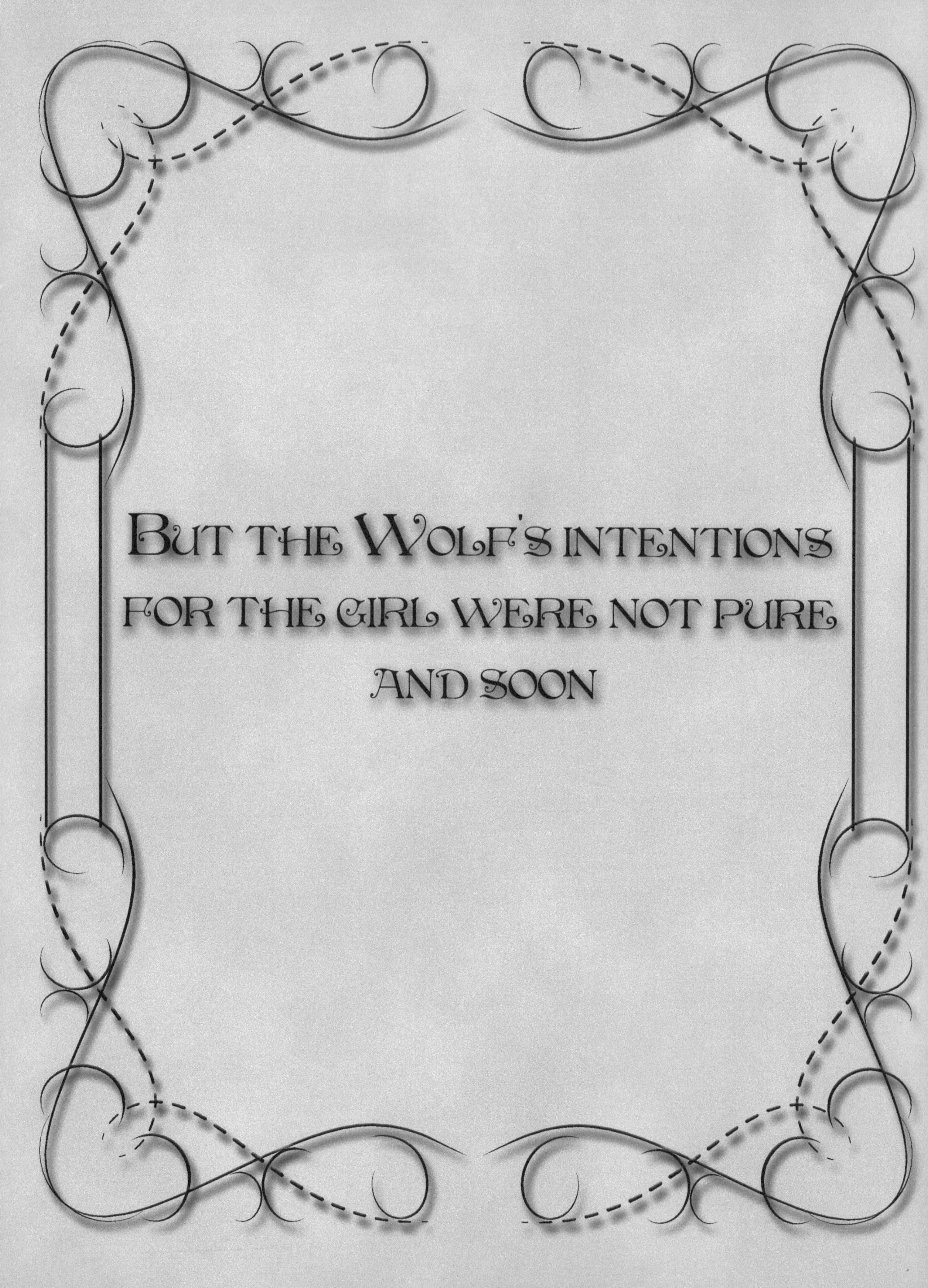

But the Wolf's intentions
for the girl were not pure
and soon

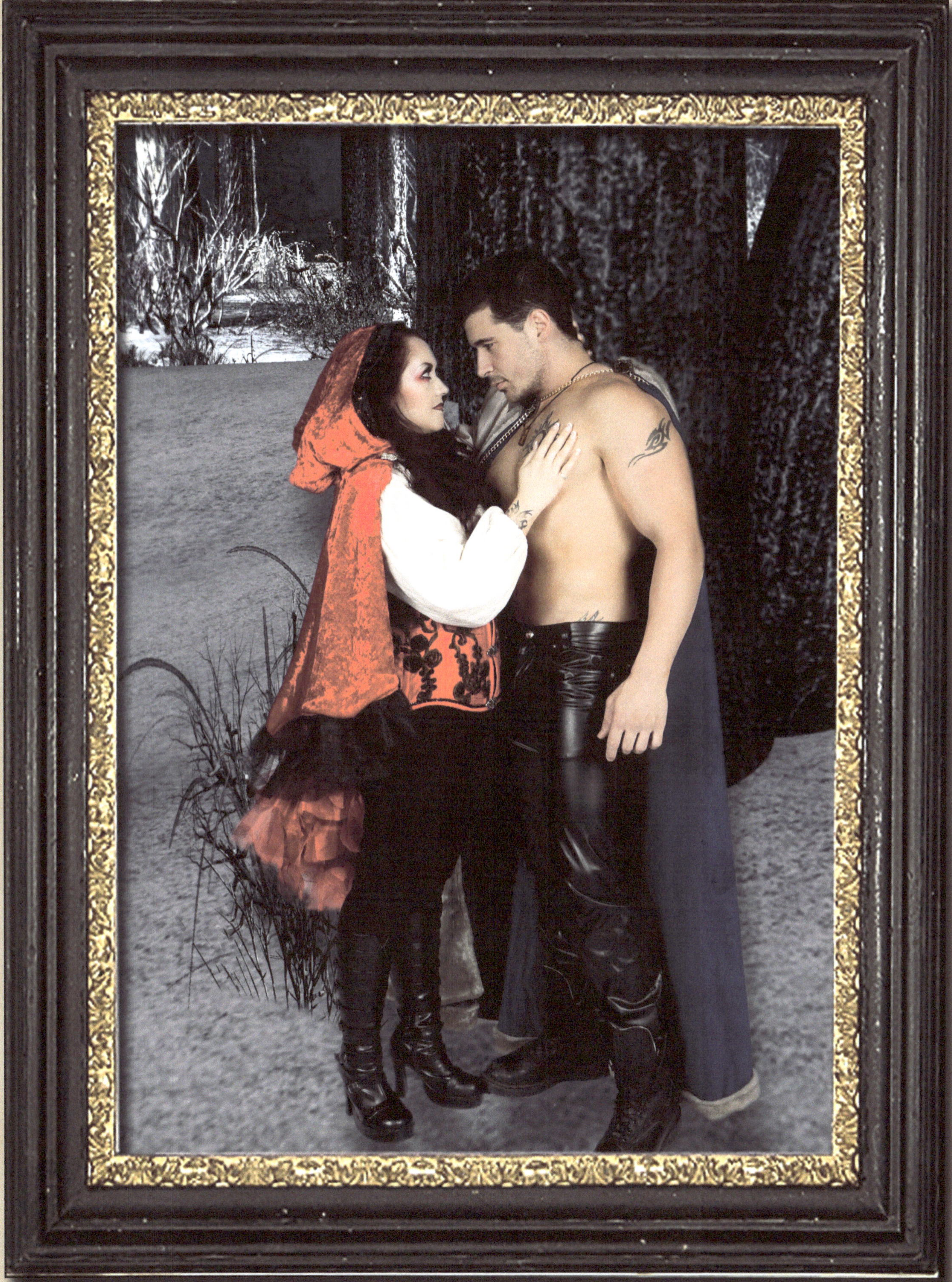

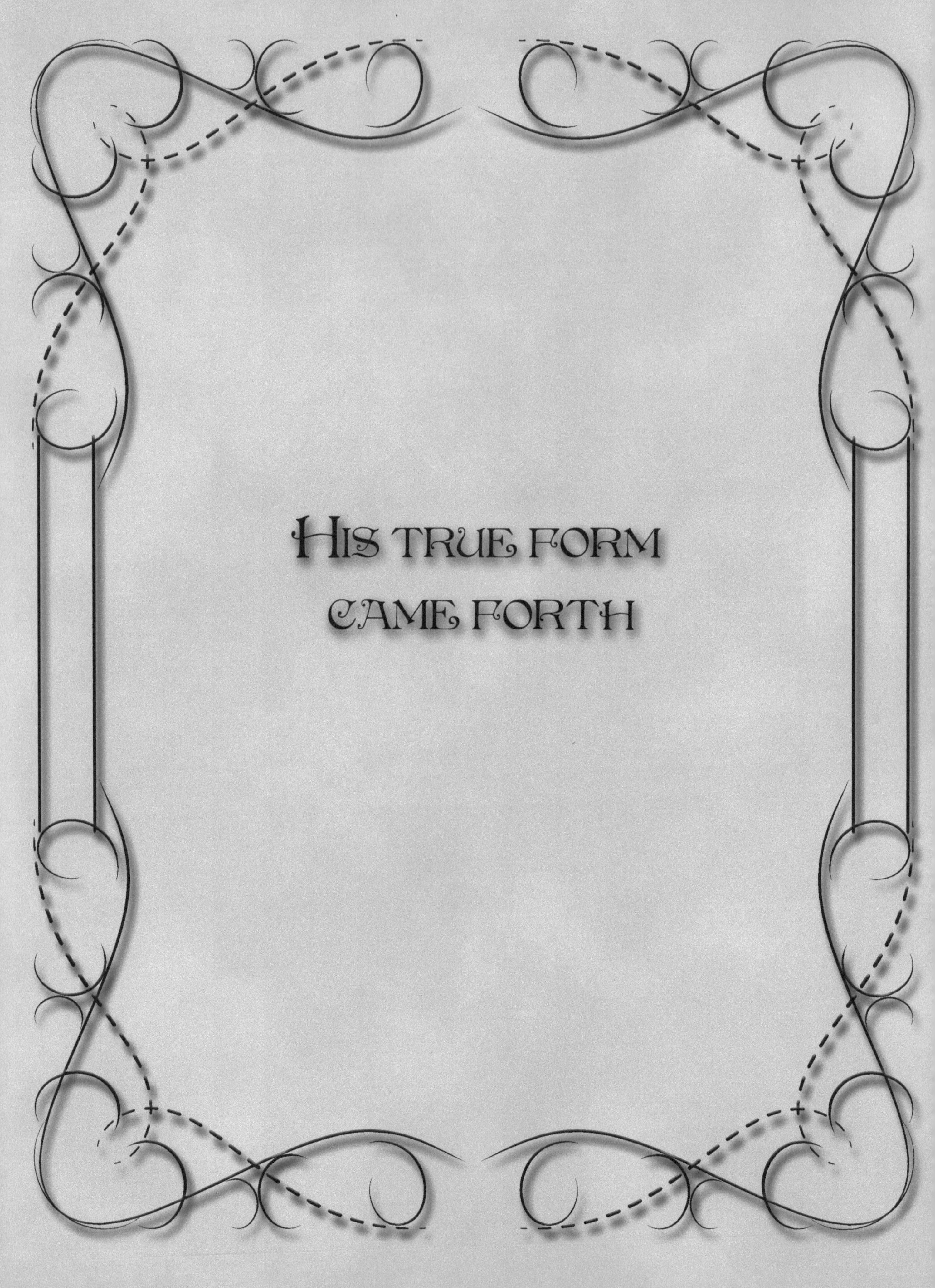

HIS TRUE FORM
CAME FORTH

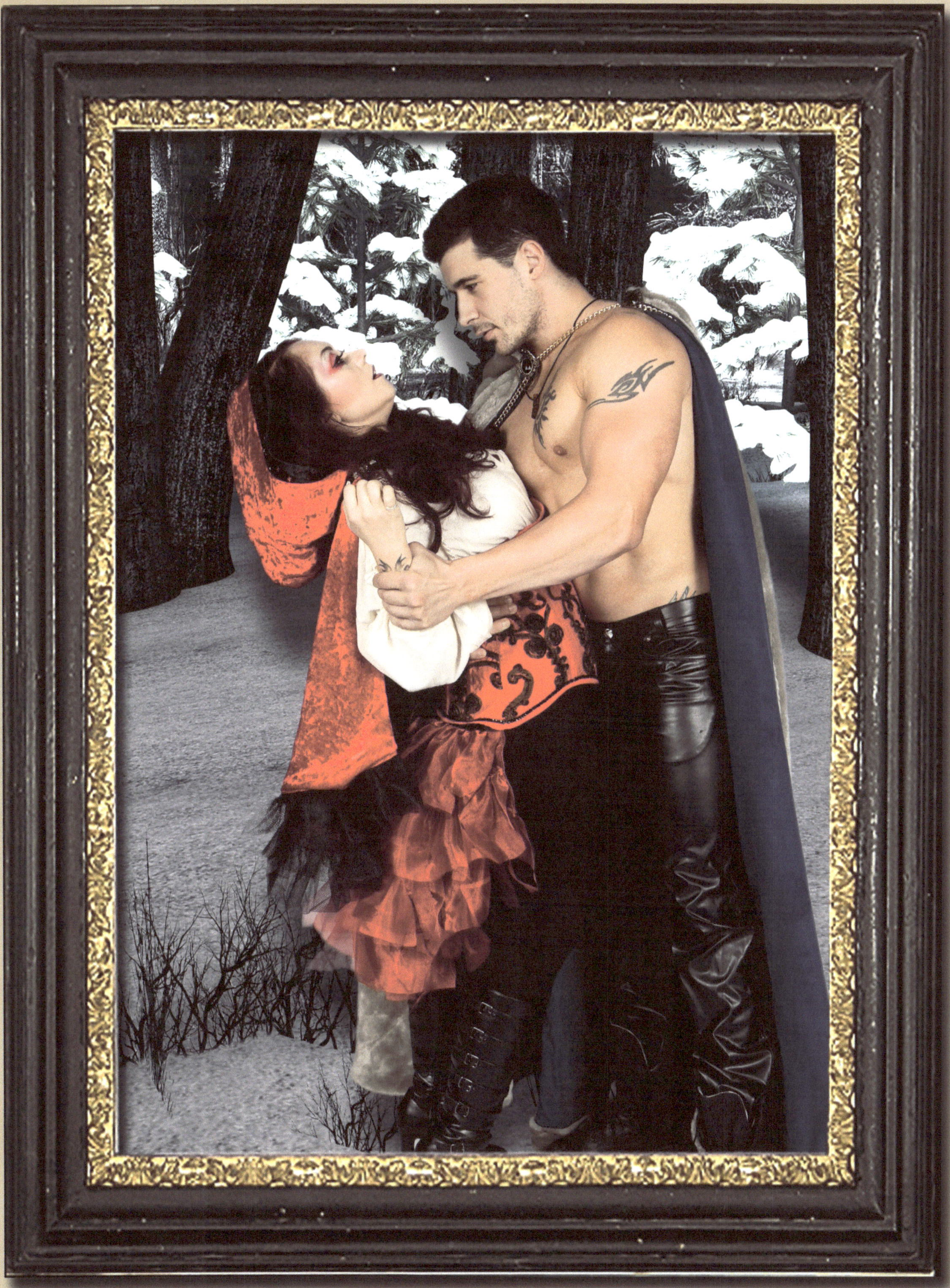

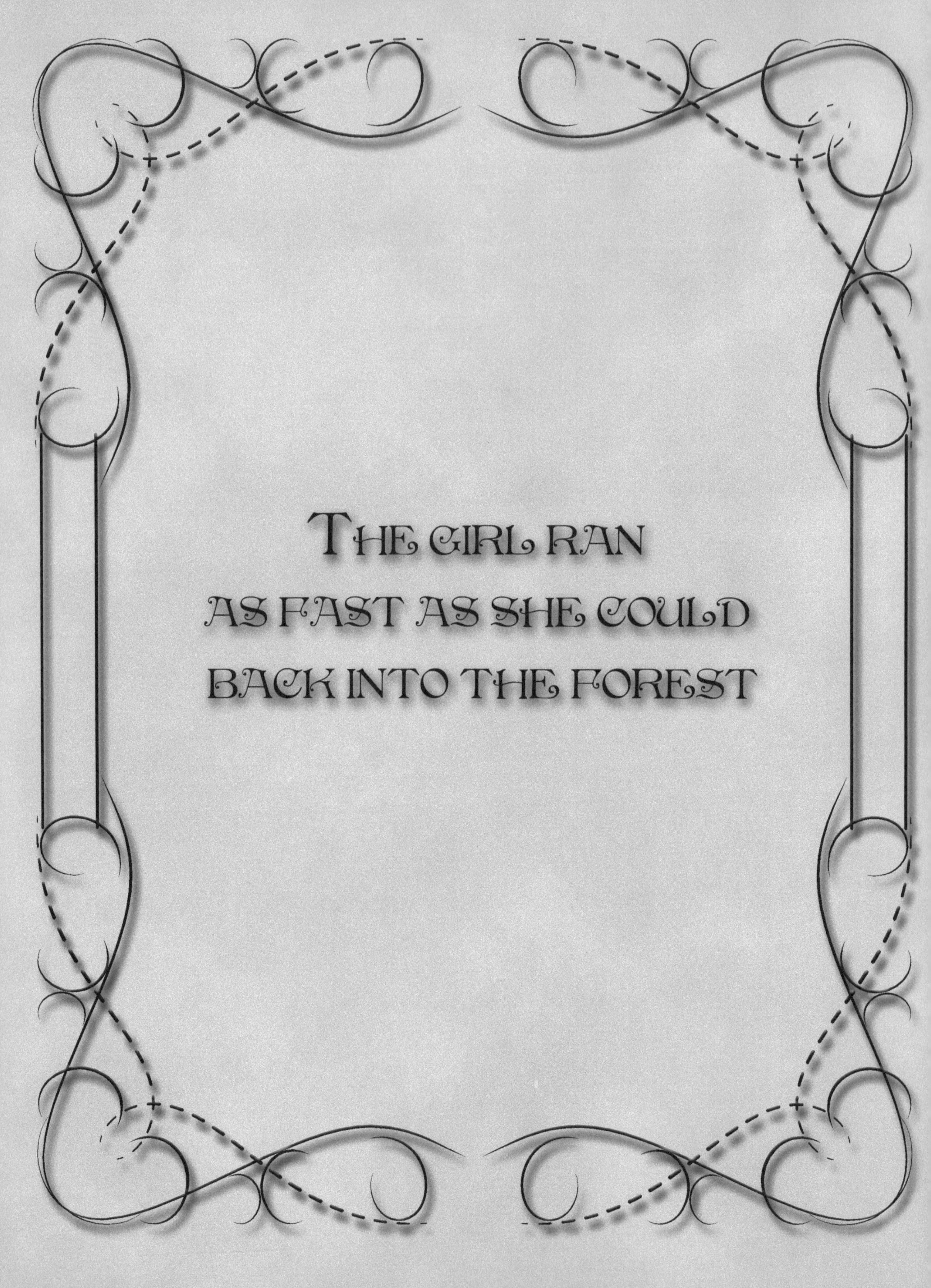

THE GIRL RAN
AS FAST AS SHE COULD
BACK INTO THE FOREST

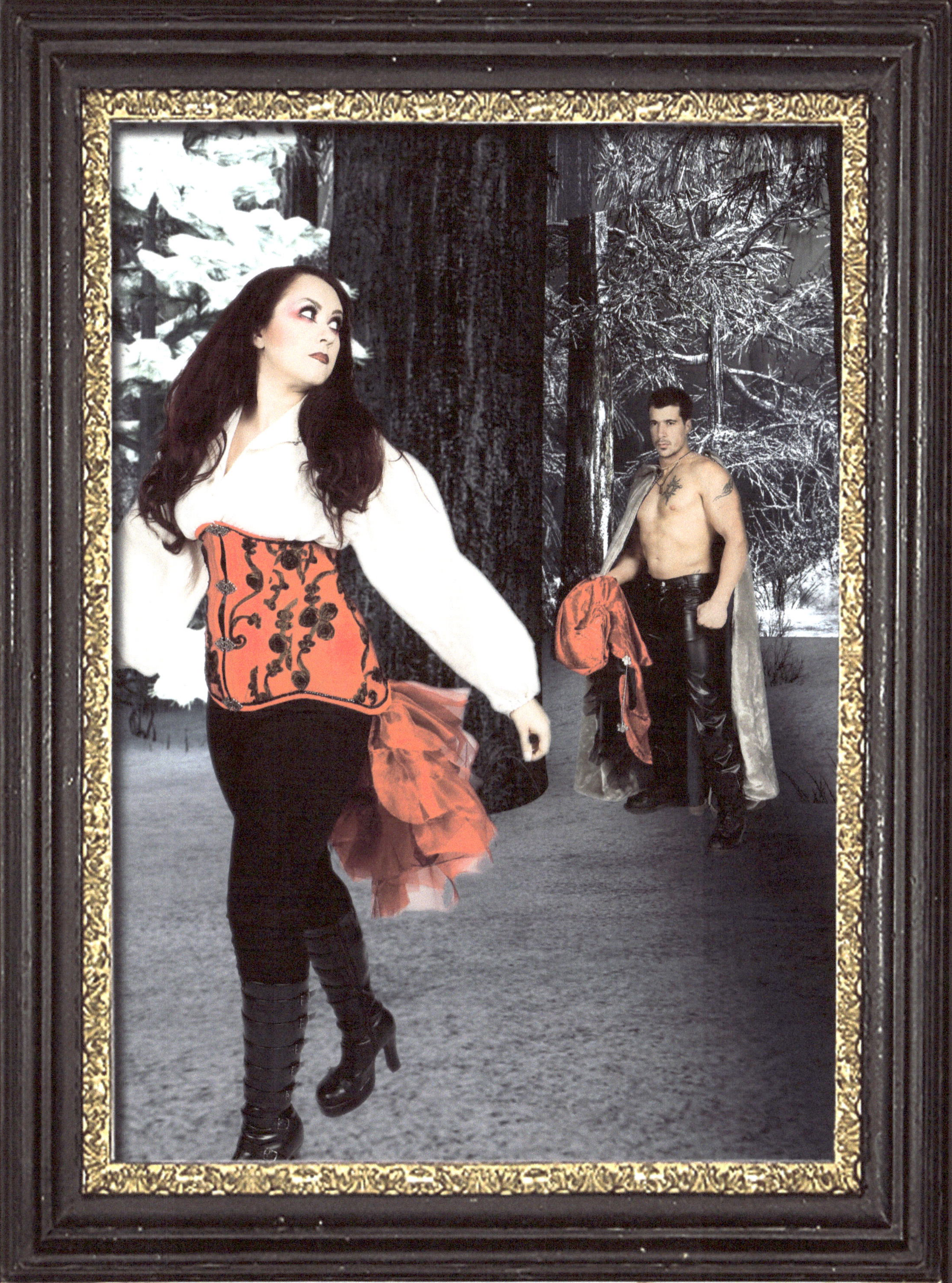

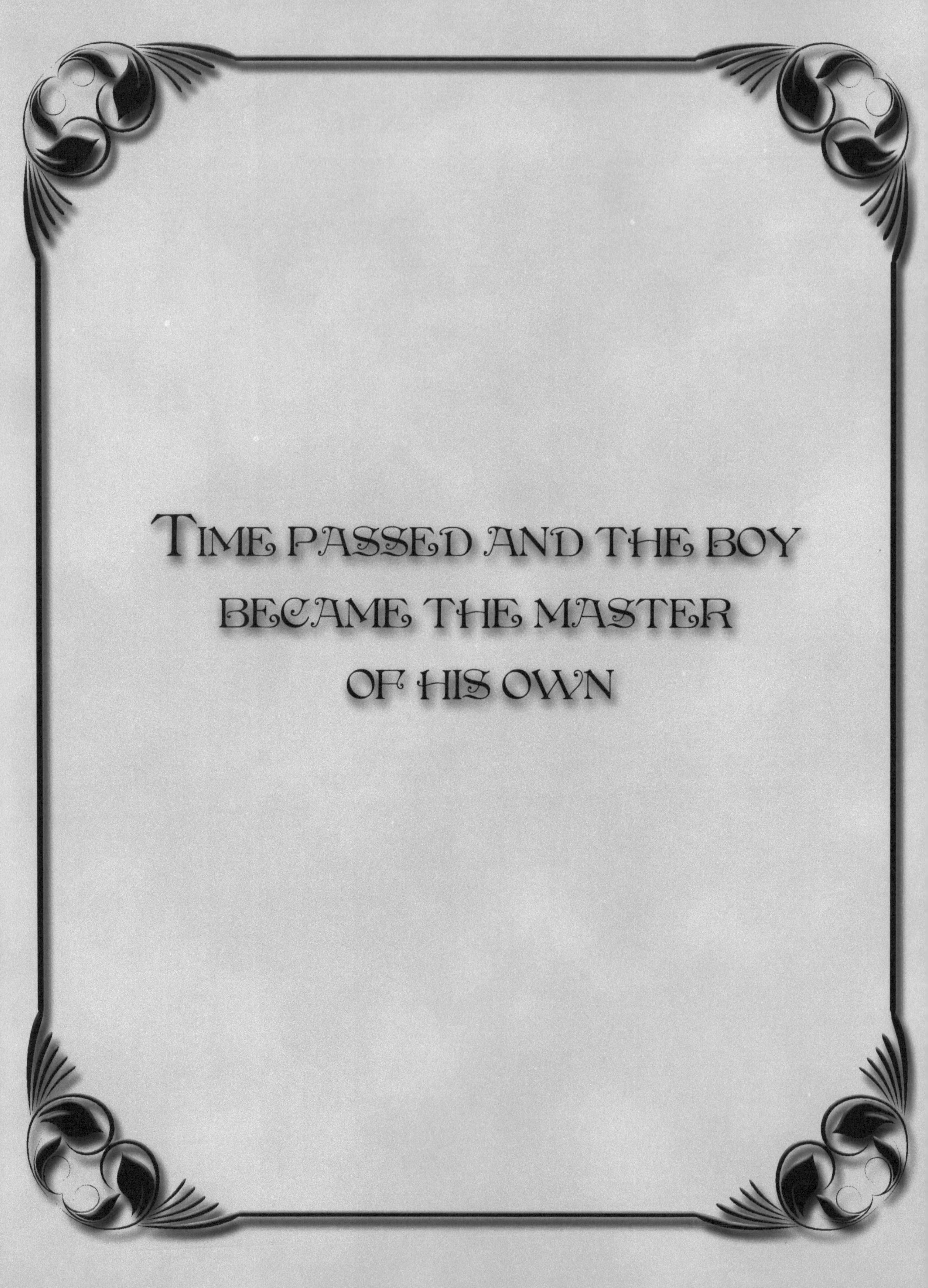

Time passed and the boy
became the master
of his own

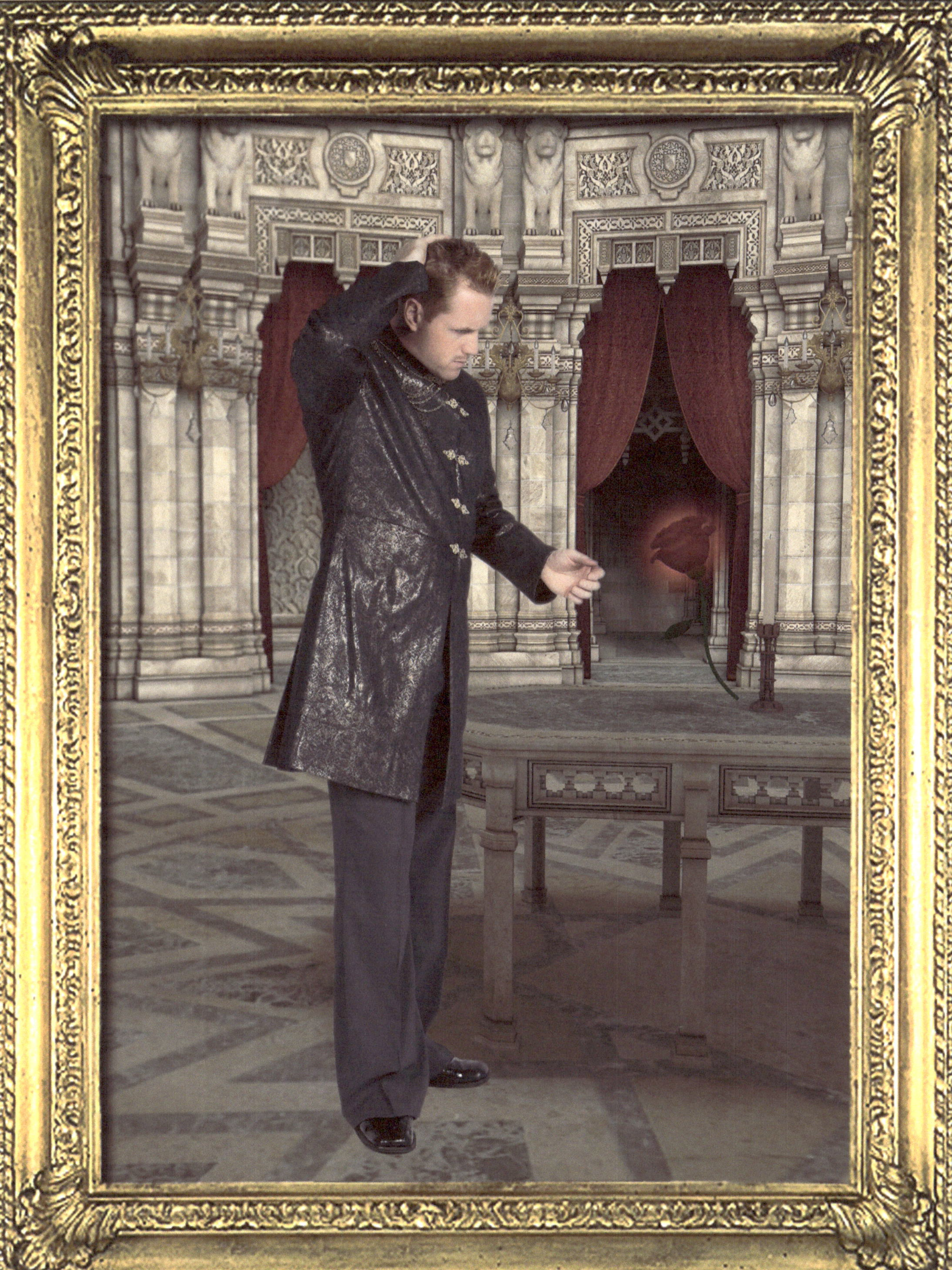

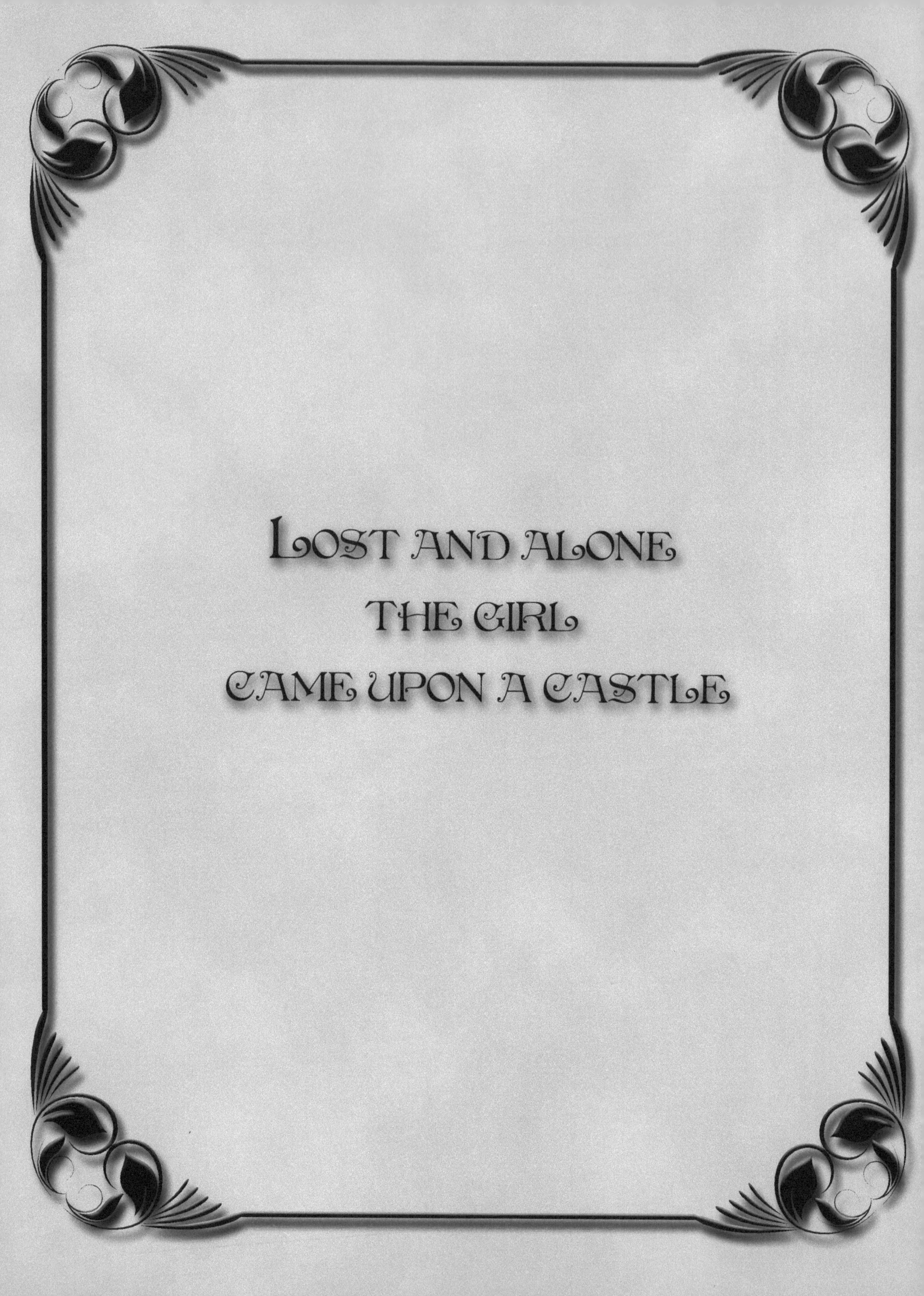

LOST AND ALONE

THE GIRL

CAME UPON A CASTLE

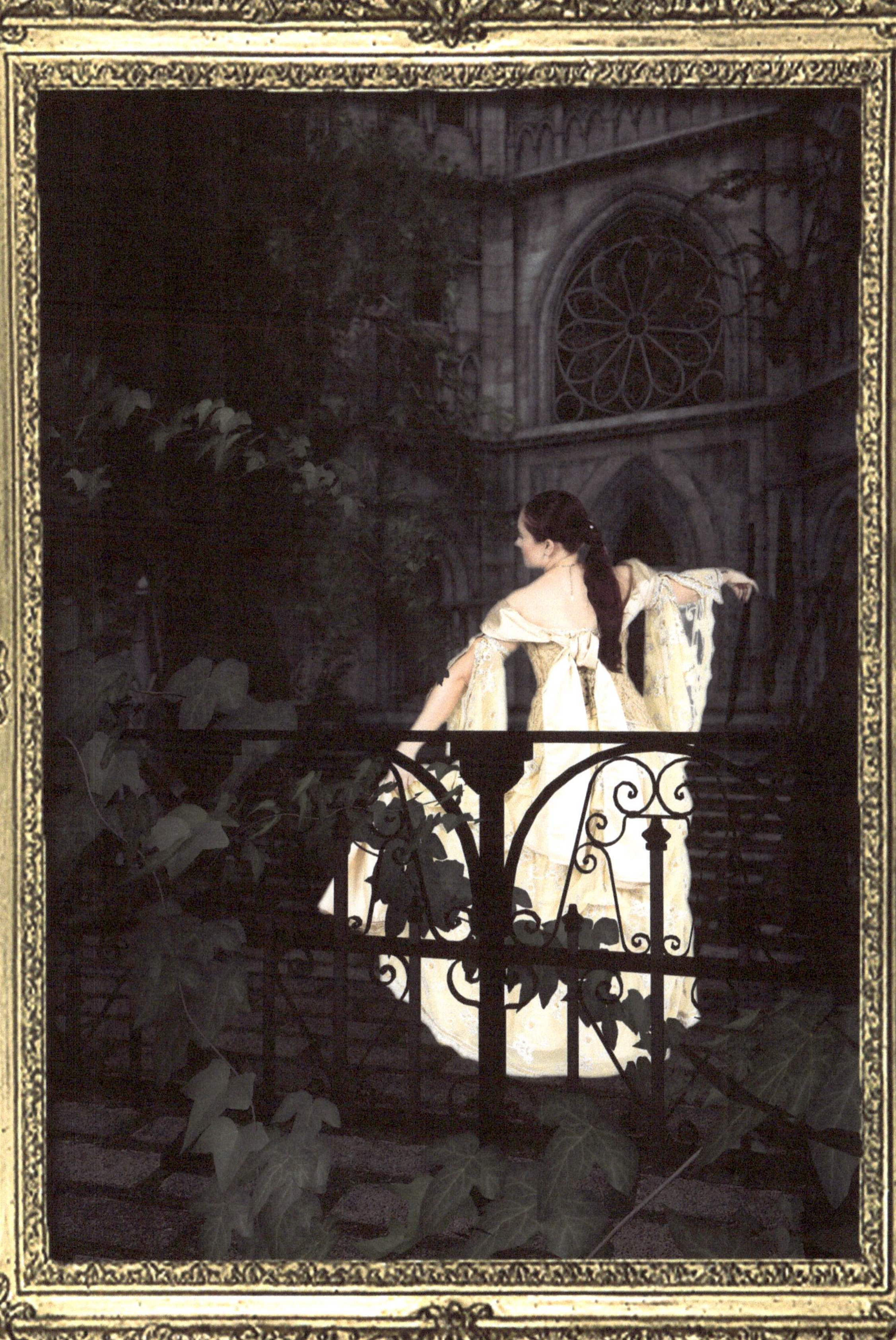

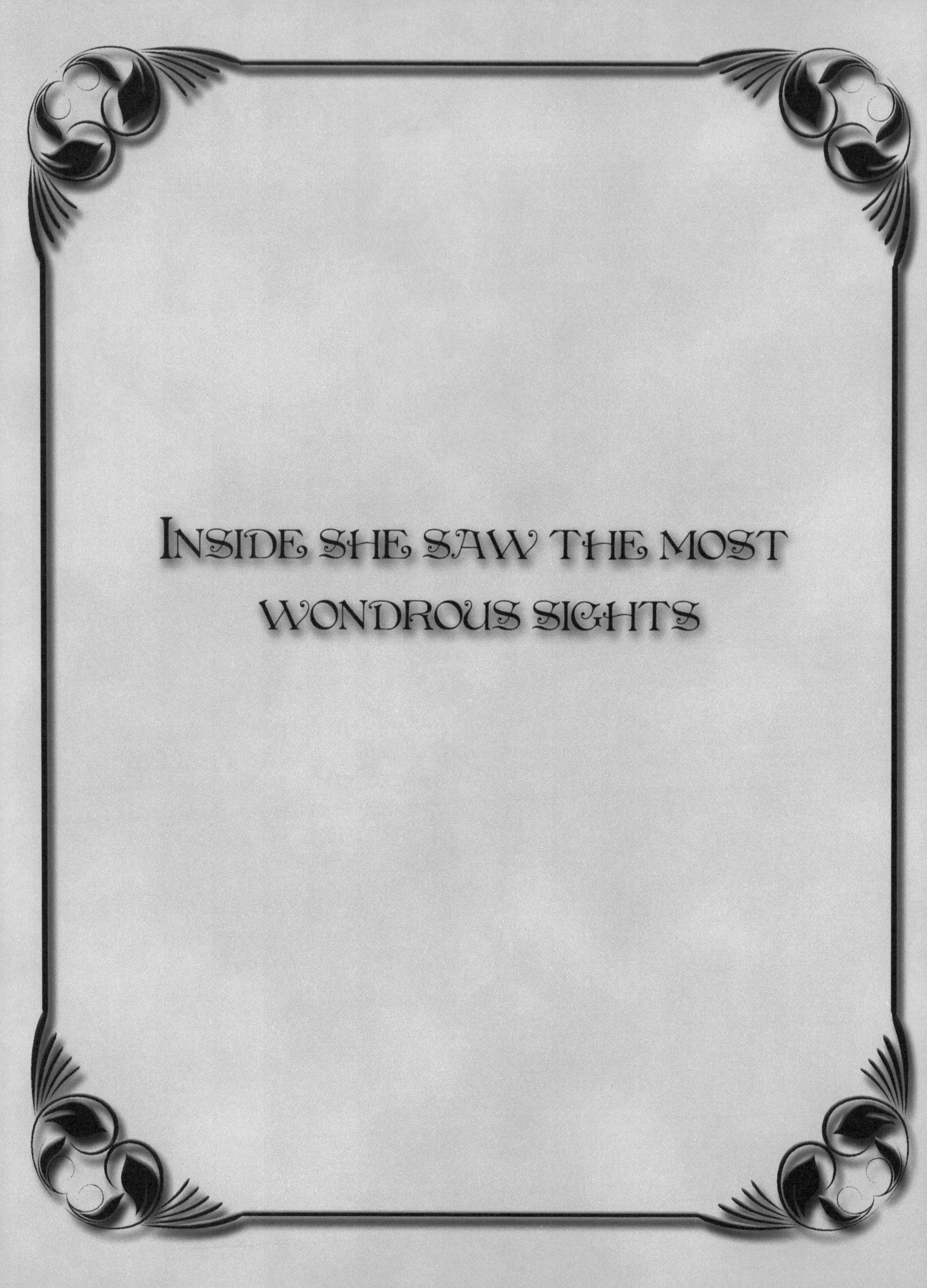

INSIDE SHE SAW THE MOST WONDROUS SIGHTS

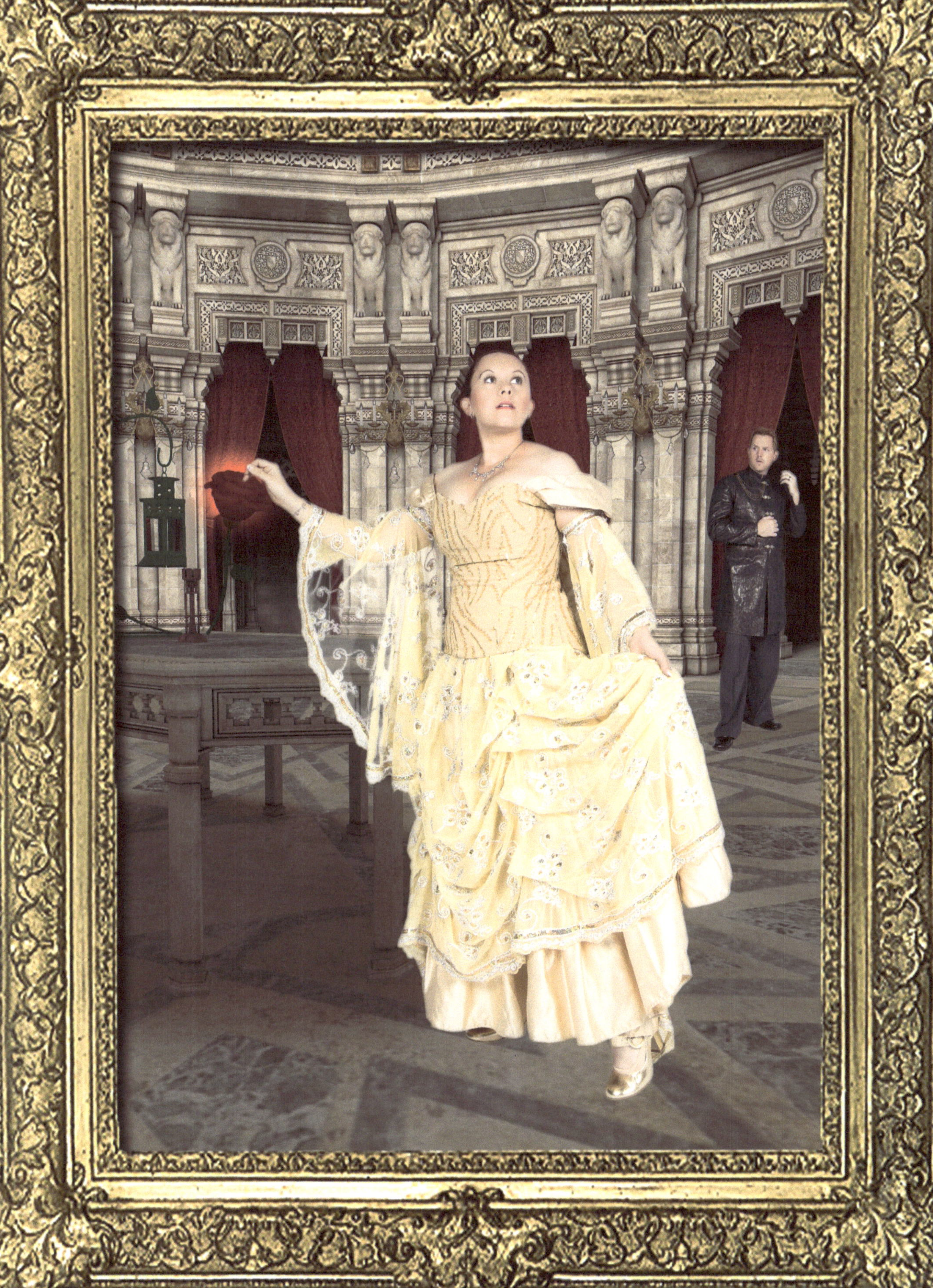

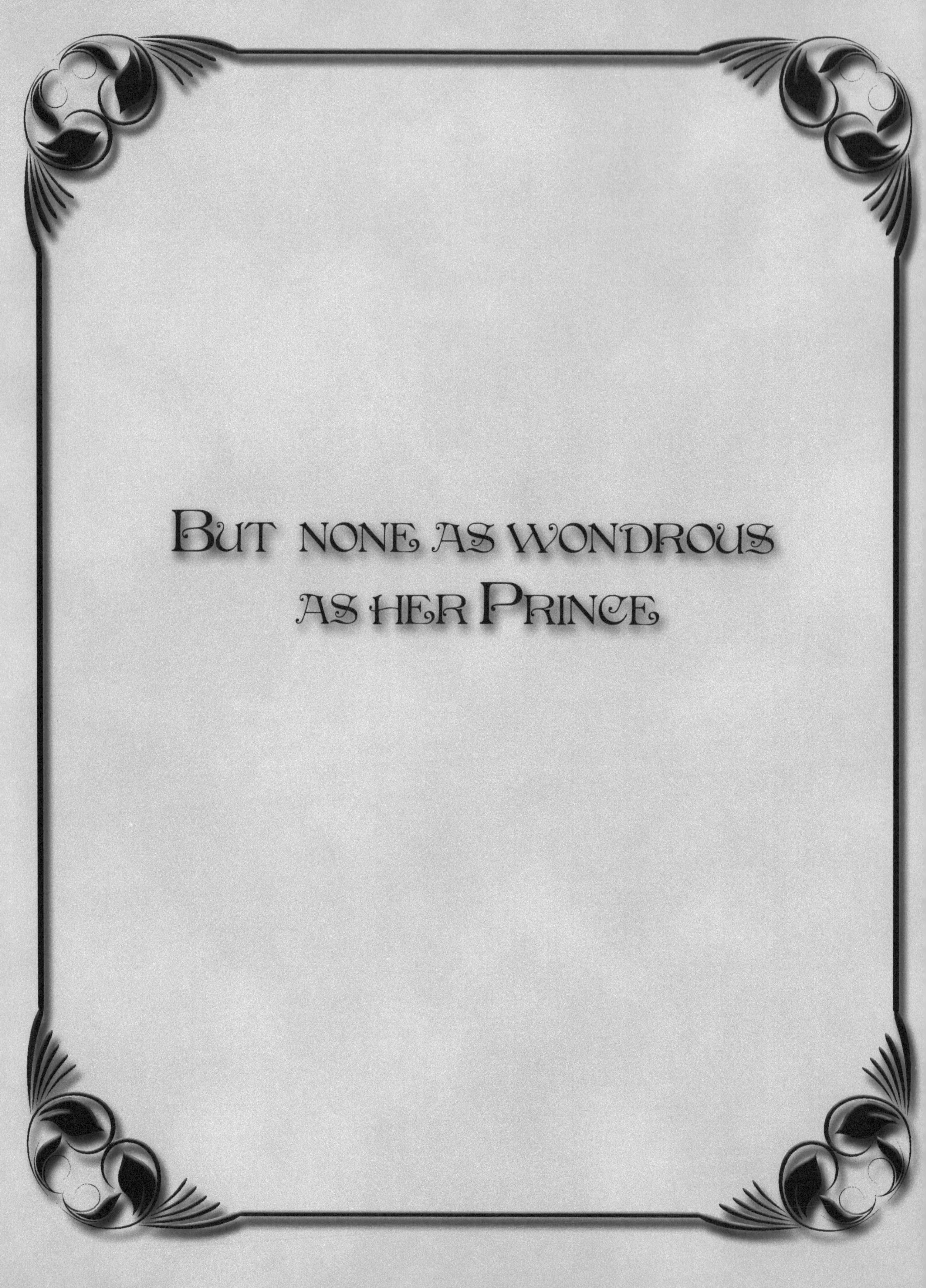
But none as wondrous
as her Prince

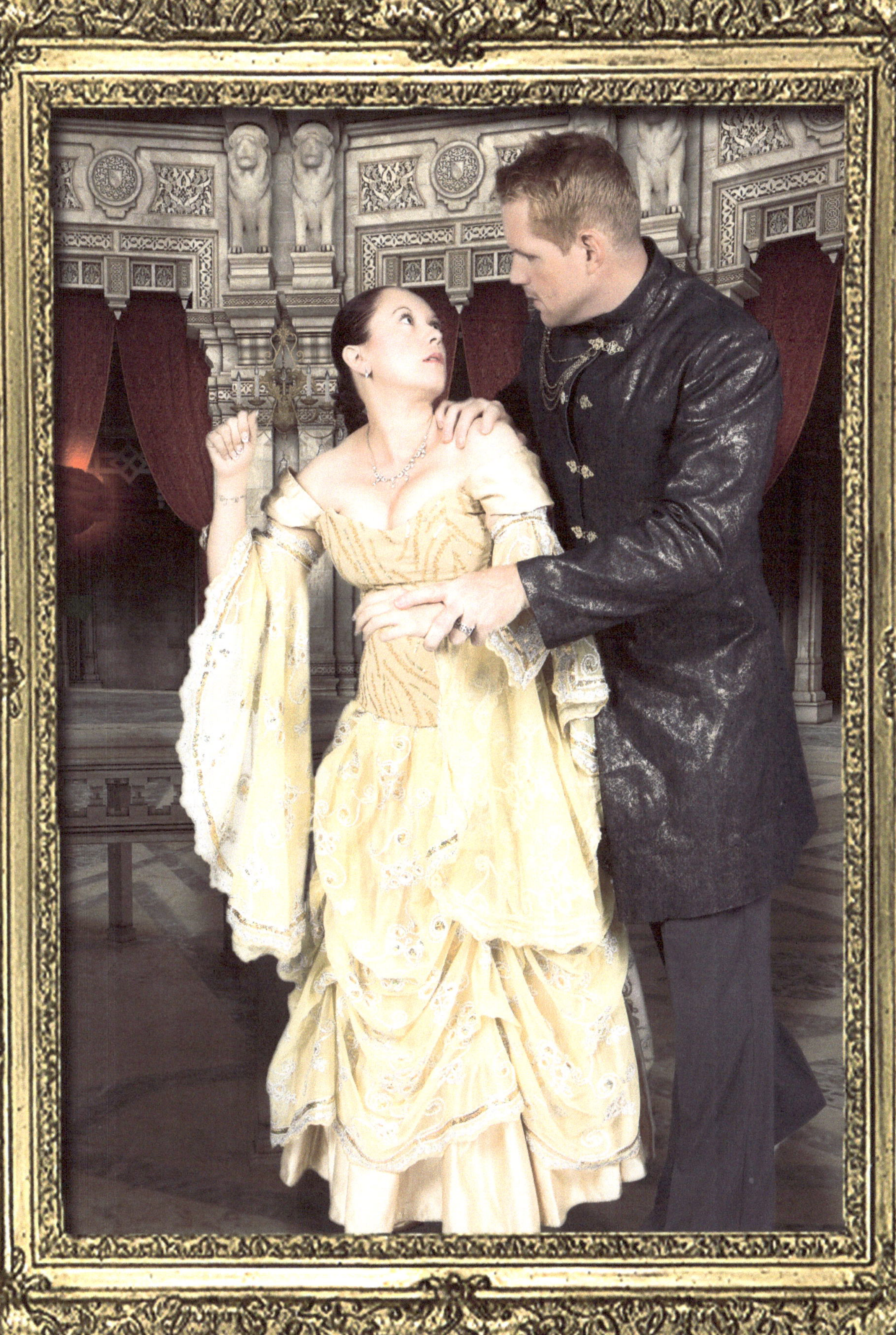

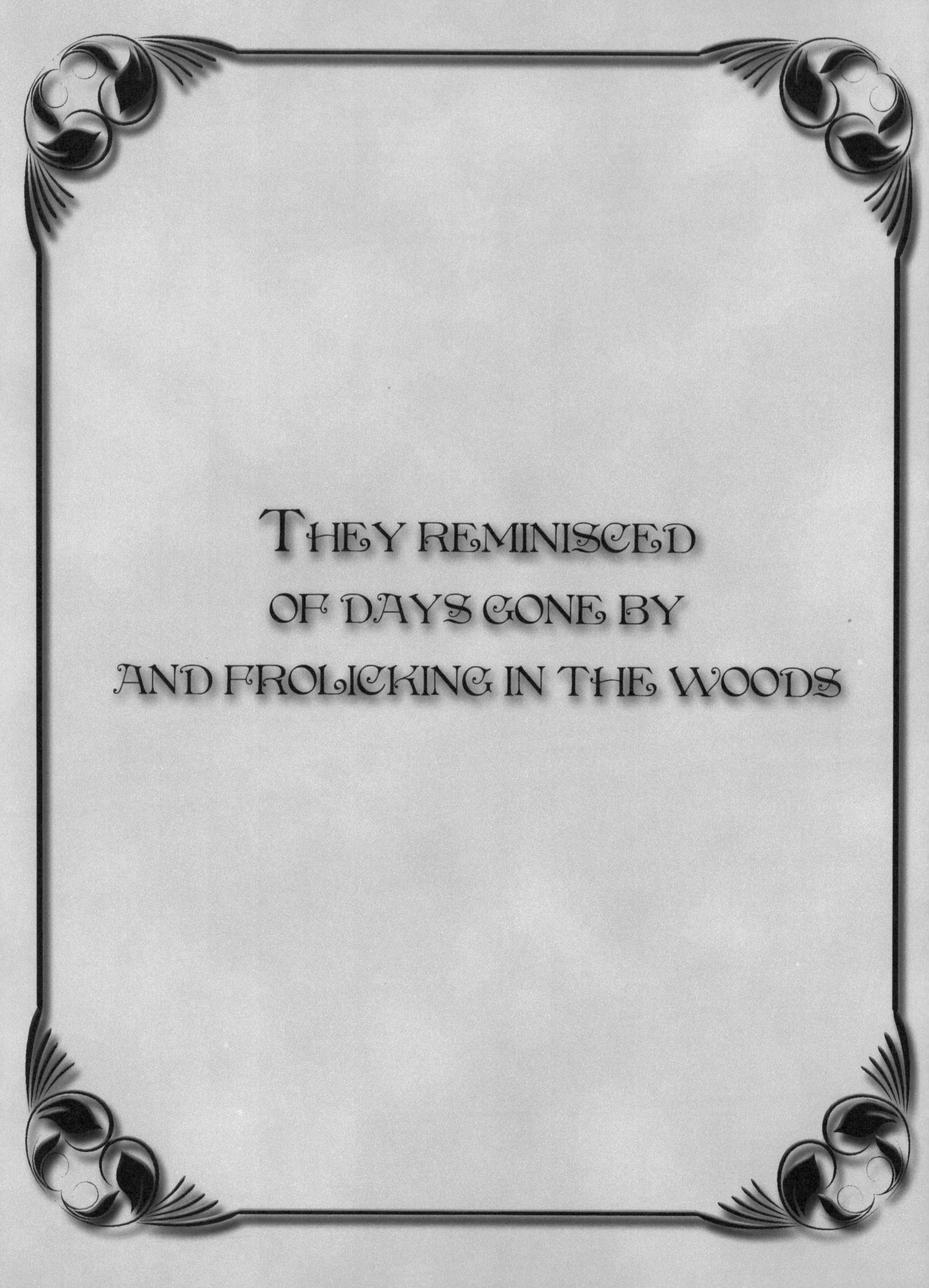
THEY REMINISCED
OF DAYS GONE BY
AND FROLICKING IN THE WOODS

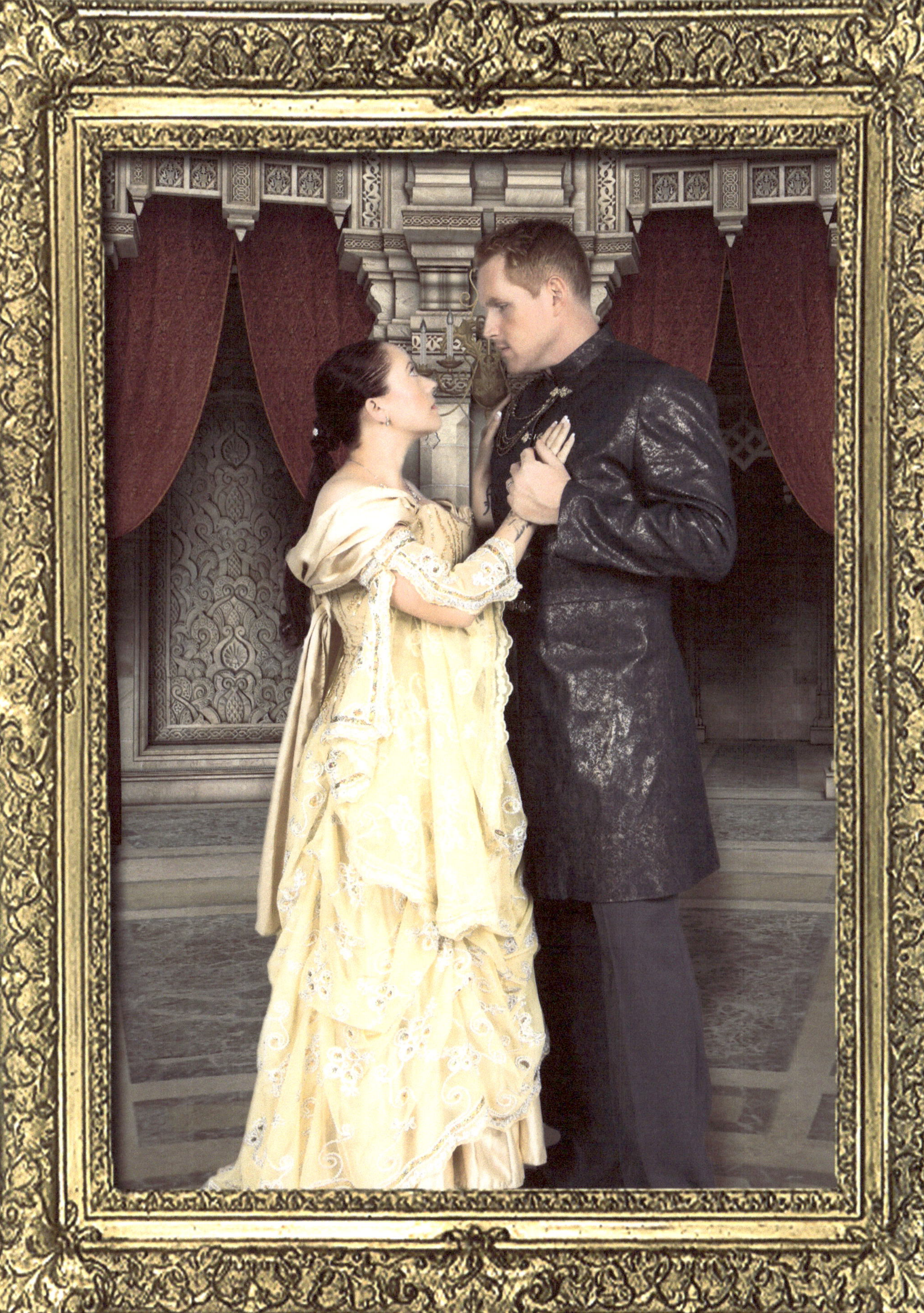

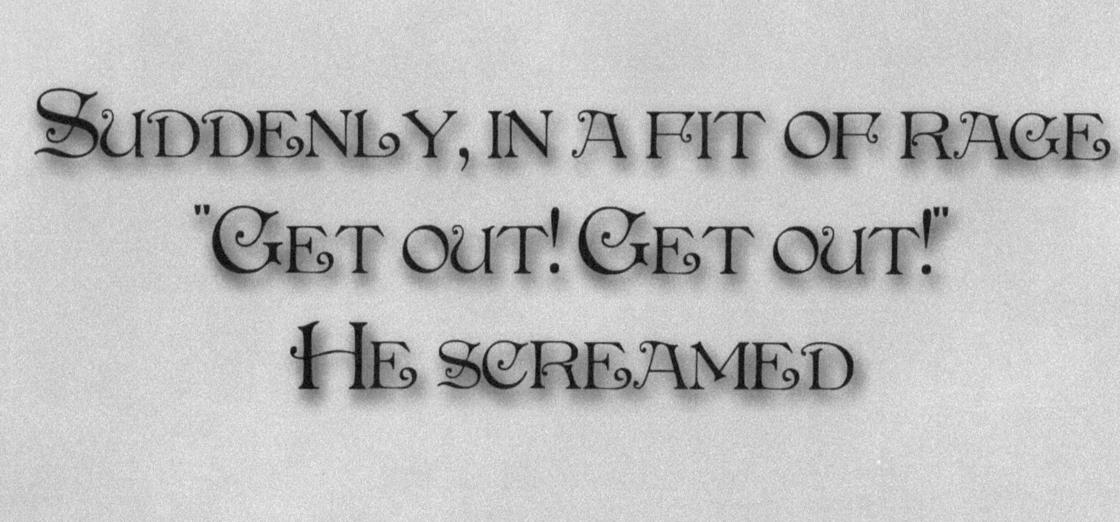
SUDDENLY, IN A FIT OF RAGE
"GET OUT! GET OUT!"
HE SCREAMED

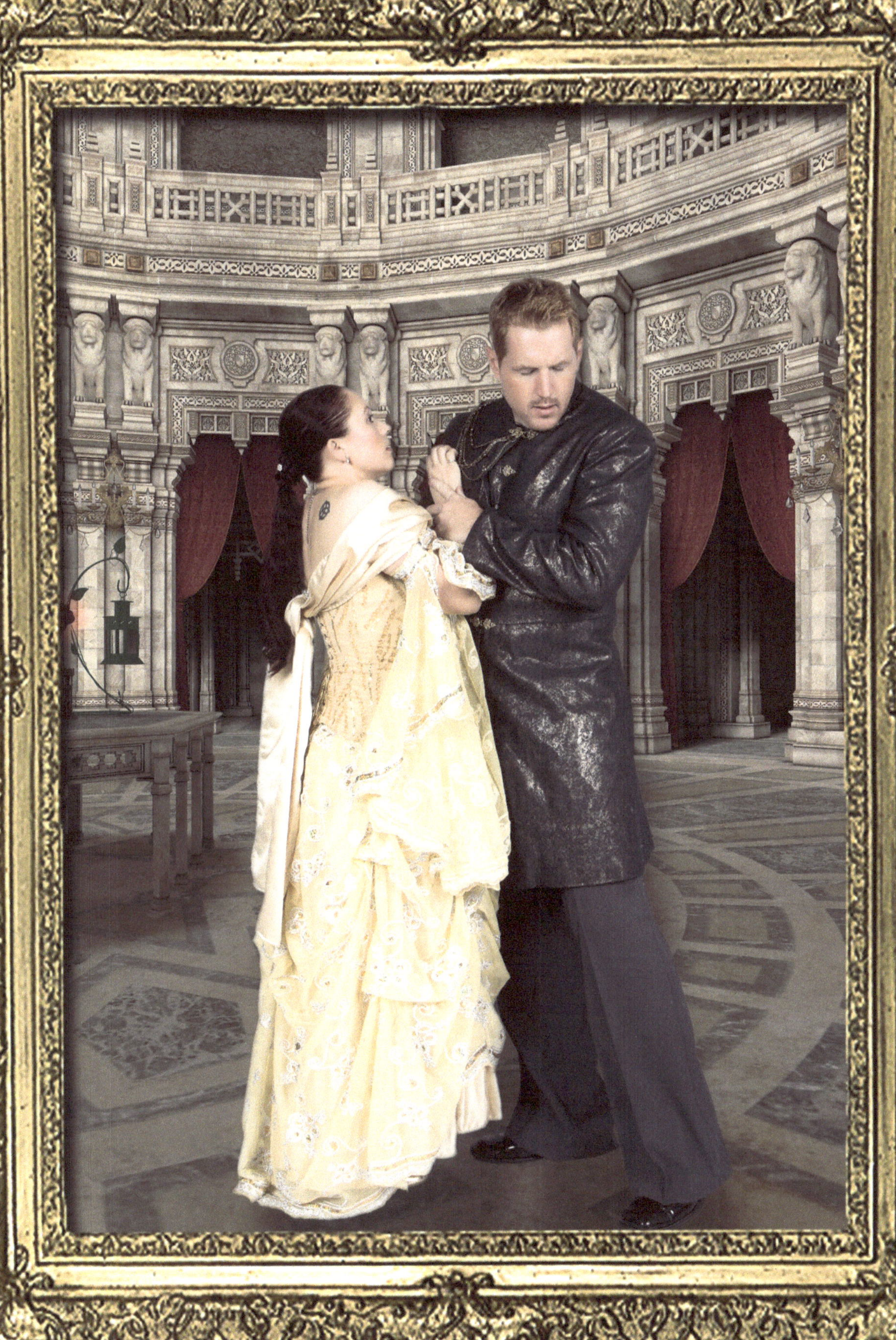

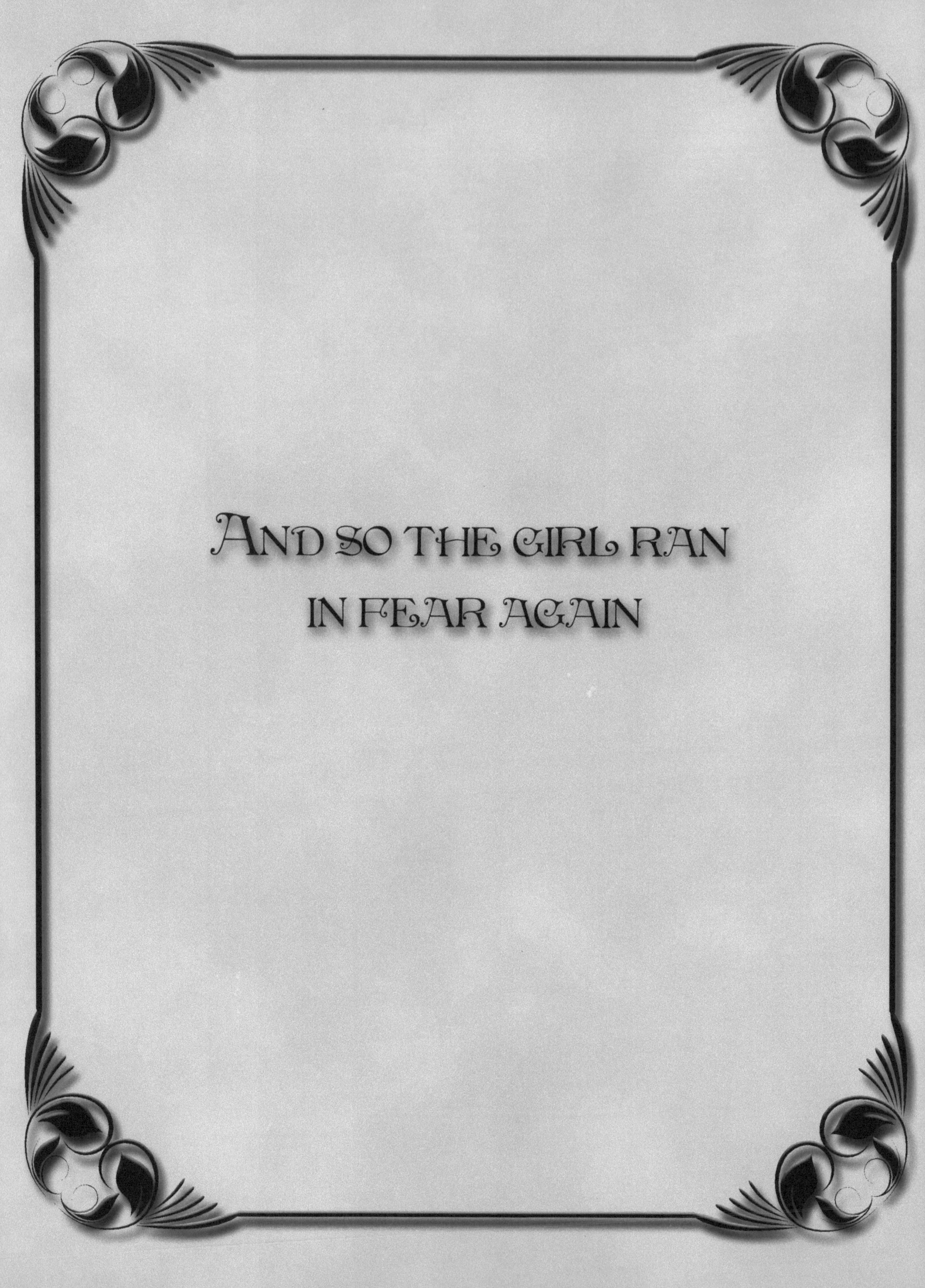

AND SO THE GIRL RAN
IN FEAR AGAIN

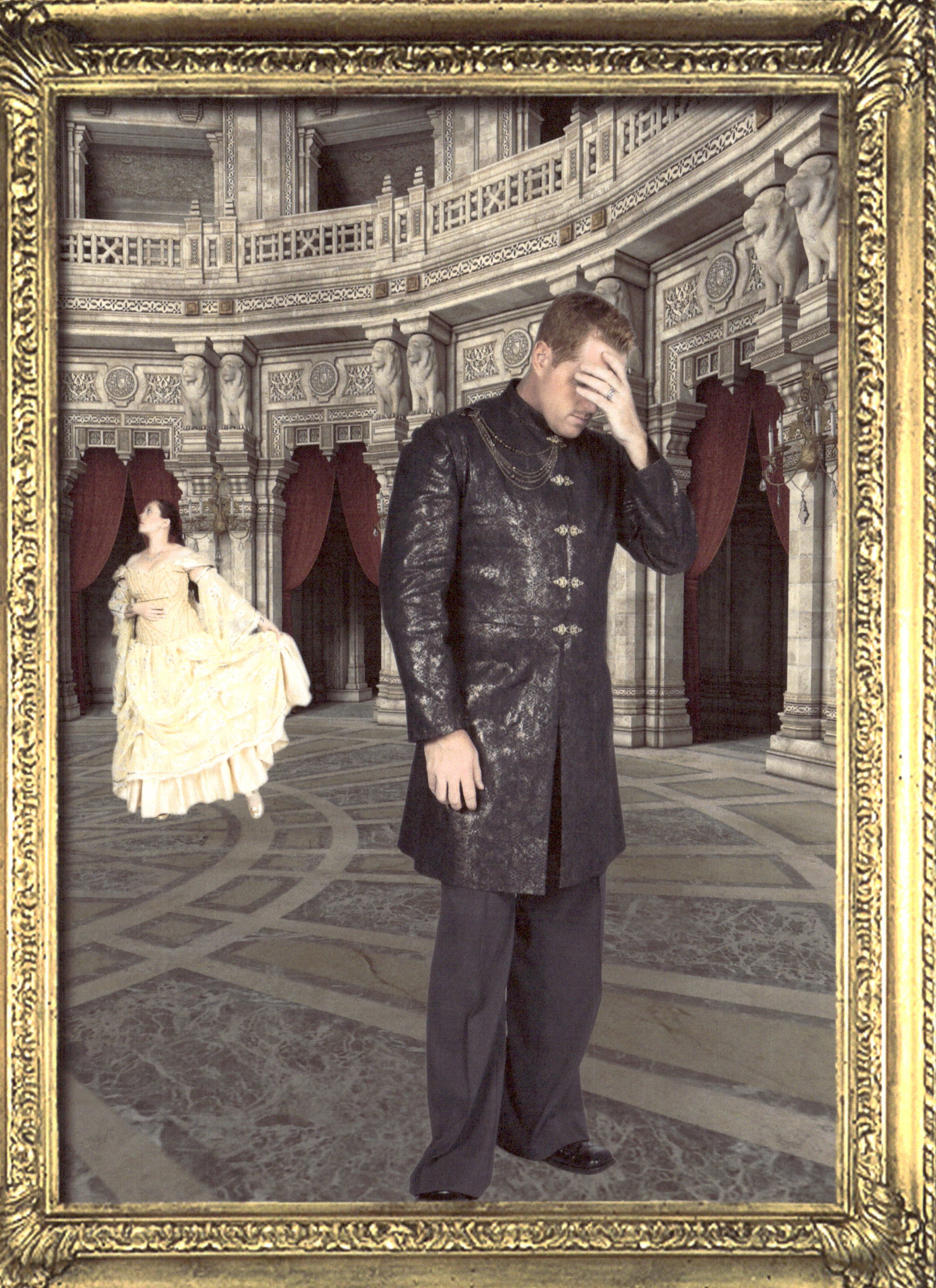

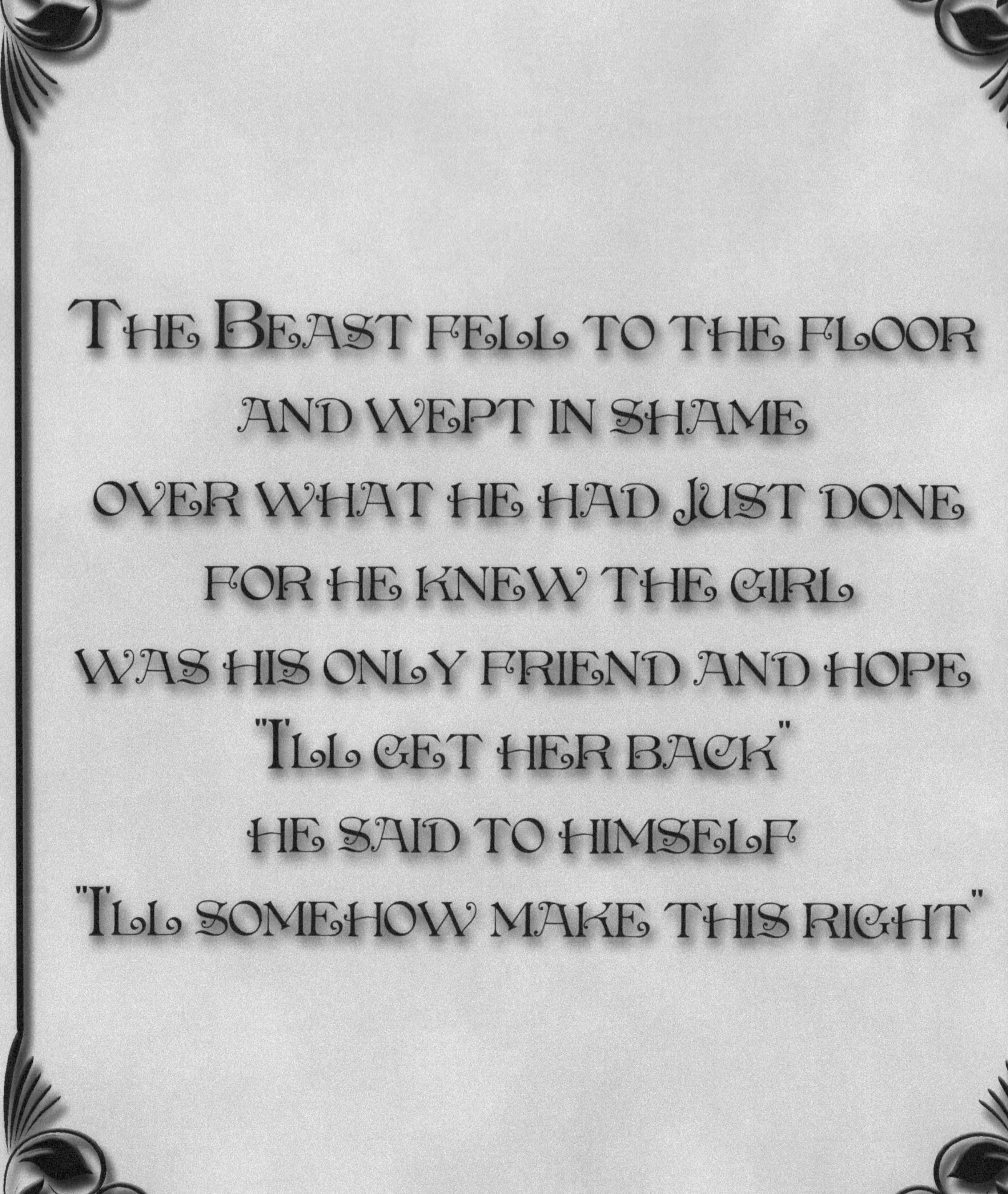

The Beast fell to the floor
and wept in shame
over what he had just done
for he knew the girl
was his only friend and hope
"I'll get her back"
he said to himself
"I'll somehow make this right"

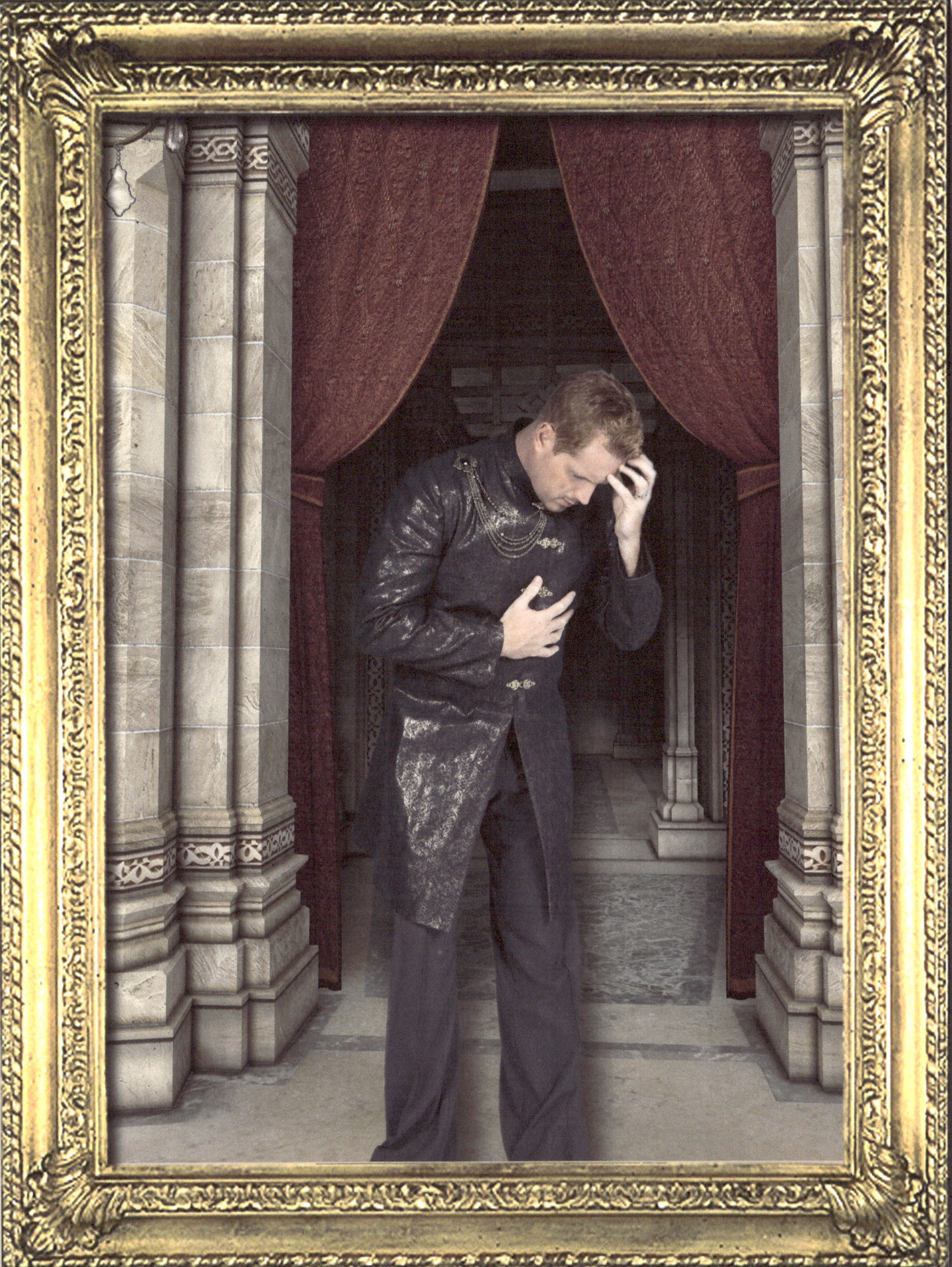

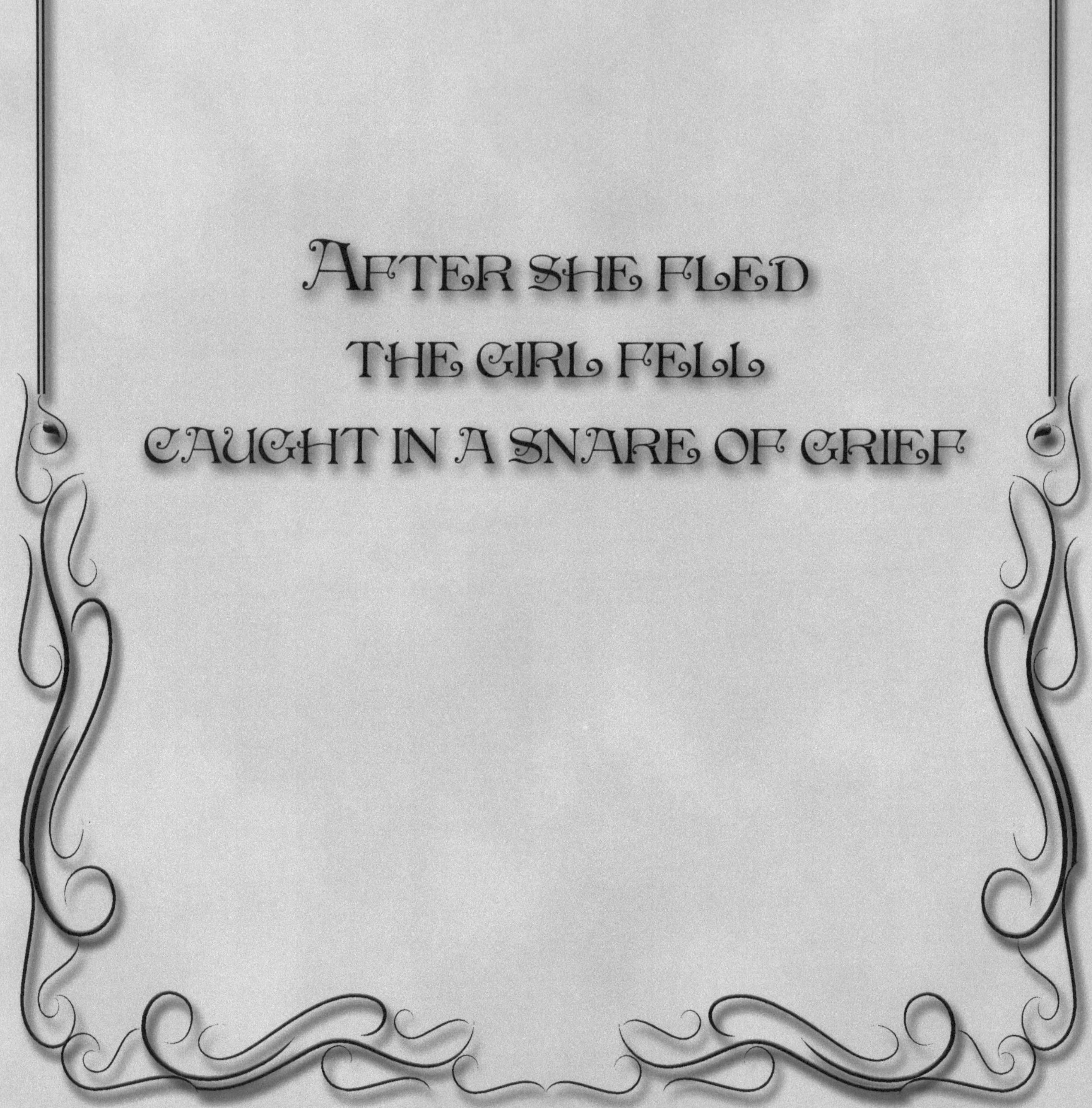

After she fled
the girl fell
caught in a snare of grief

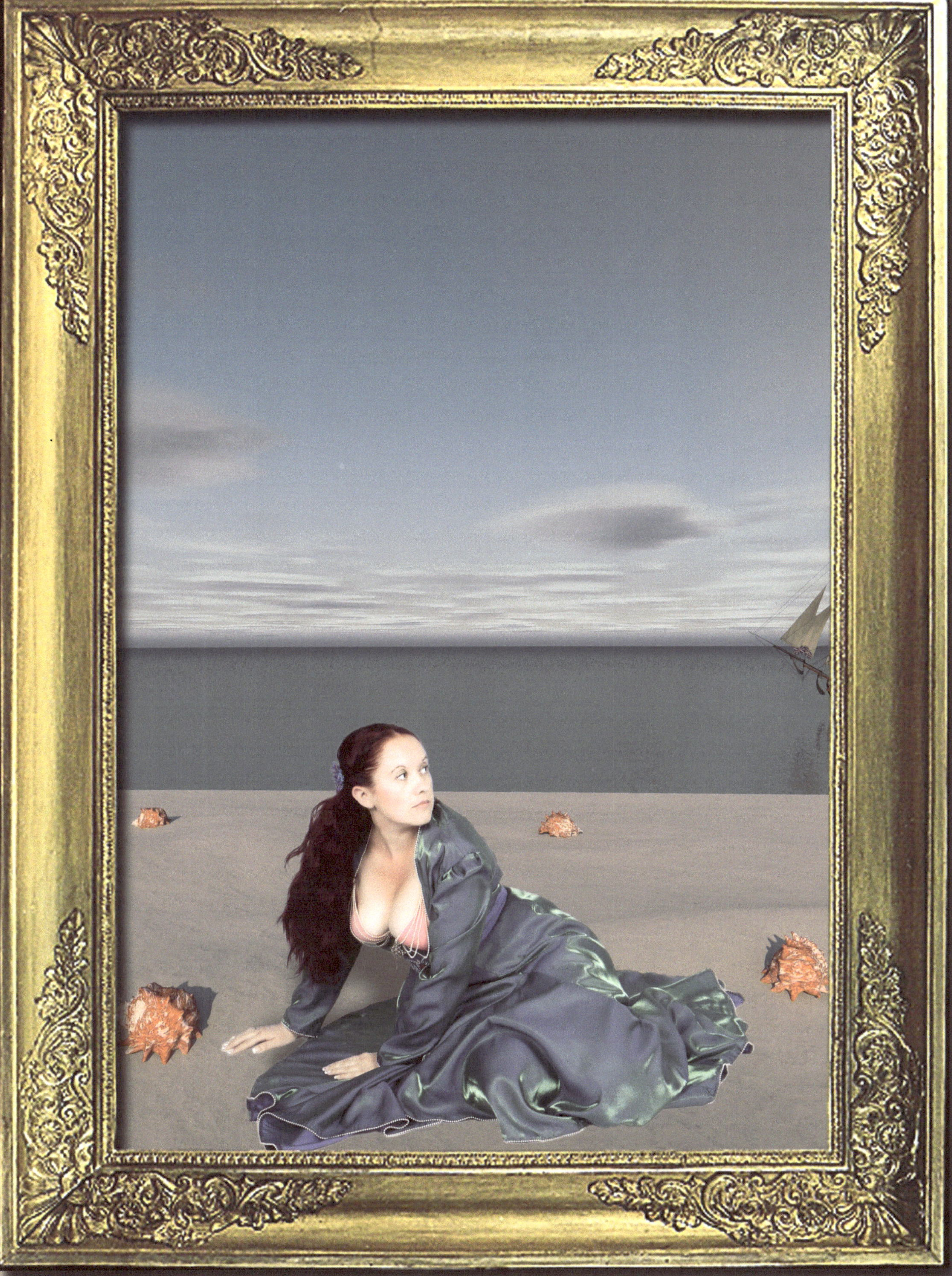

Hearing her cries
the prince came at last

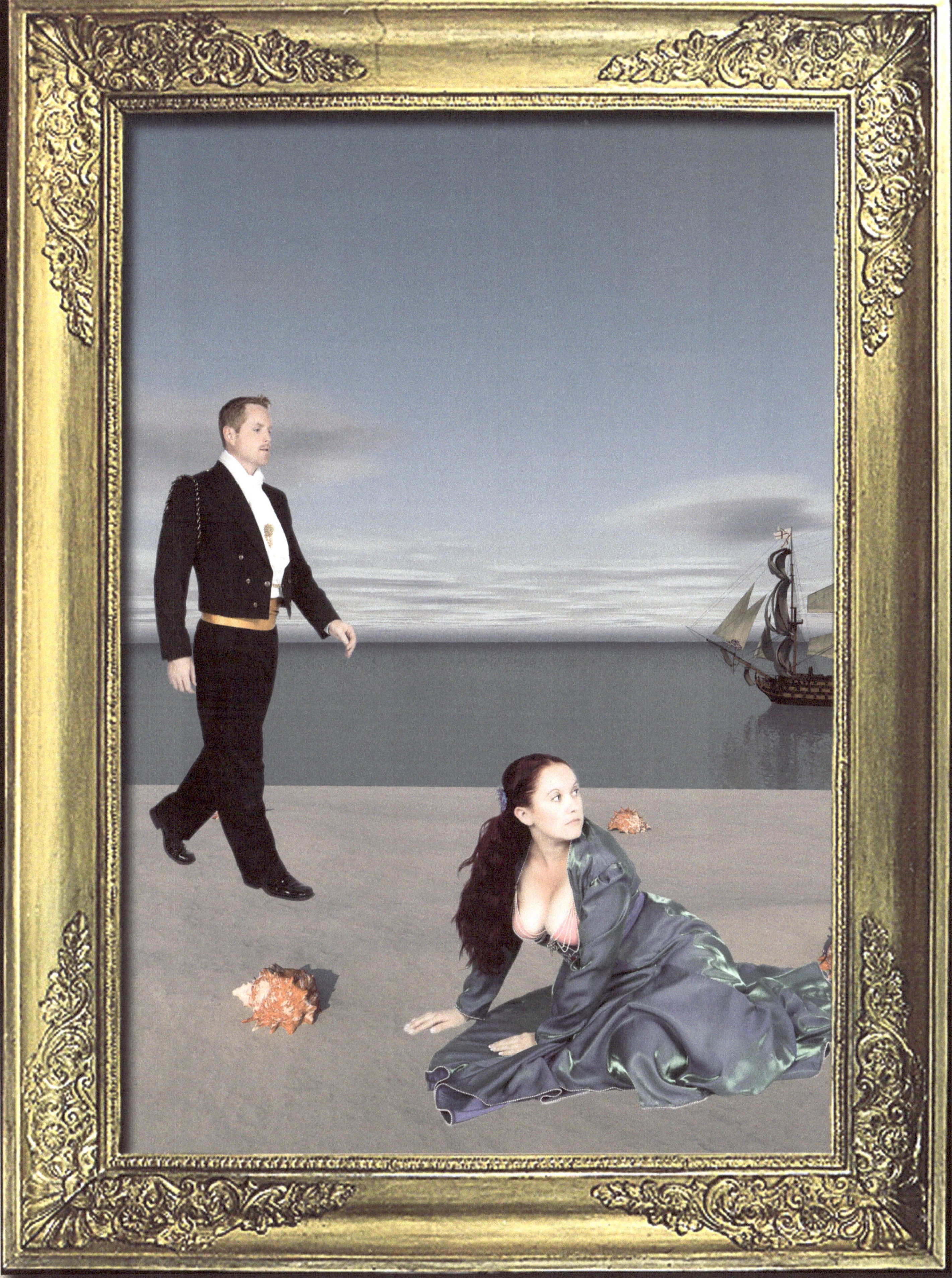

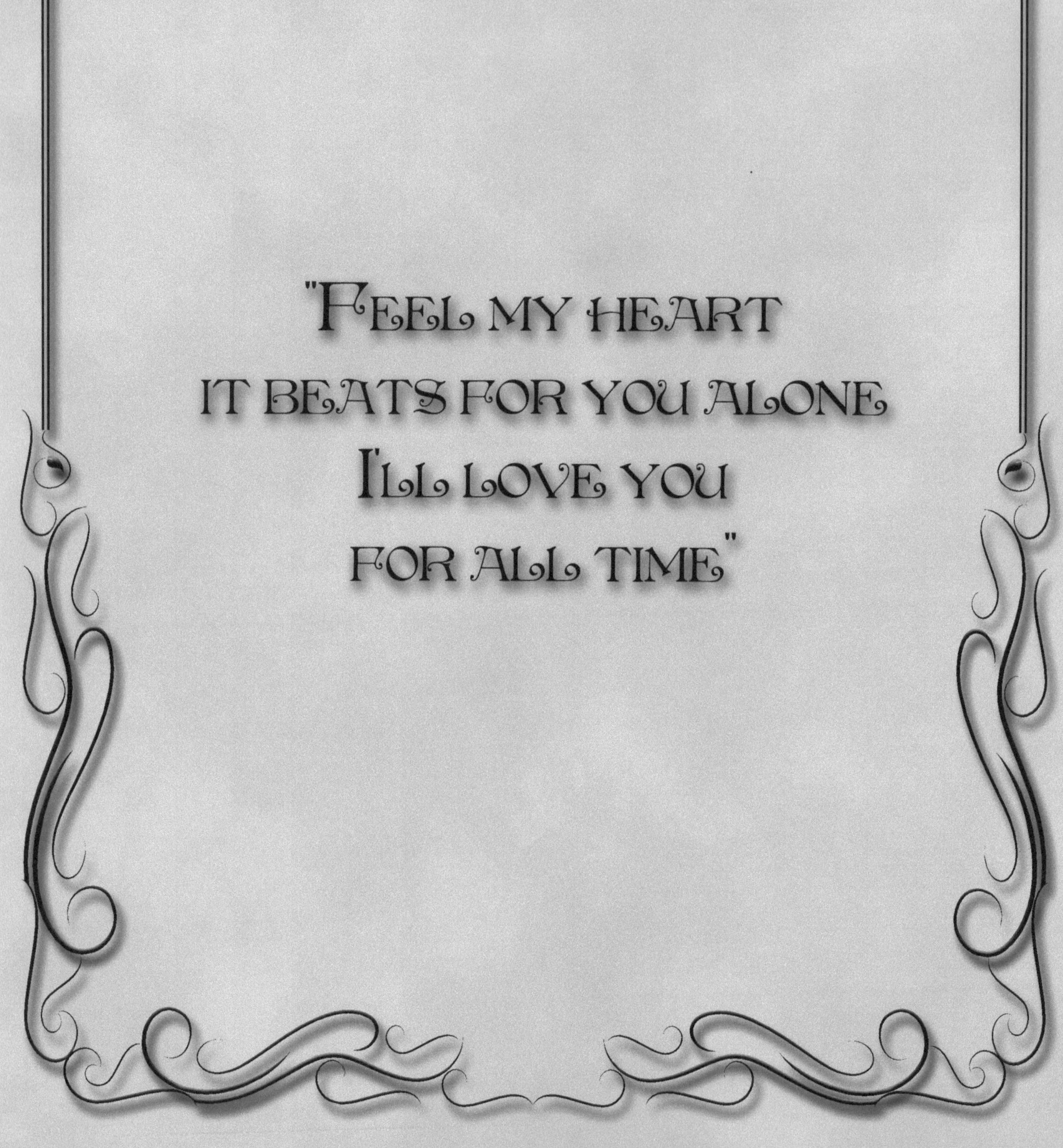
"Feel my heart
it beats for you alone
I'll love you
for all time"

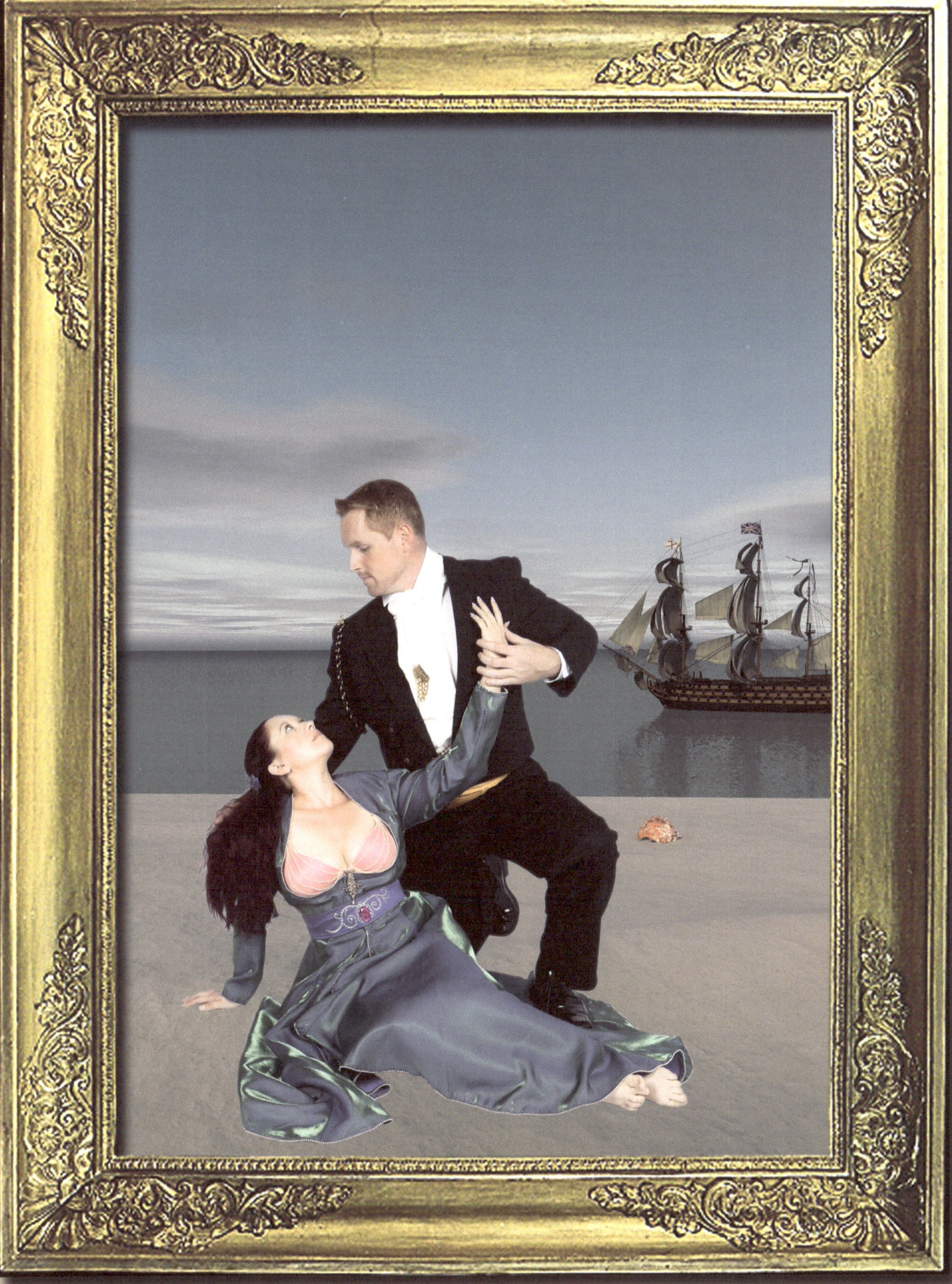

He helped her stand

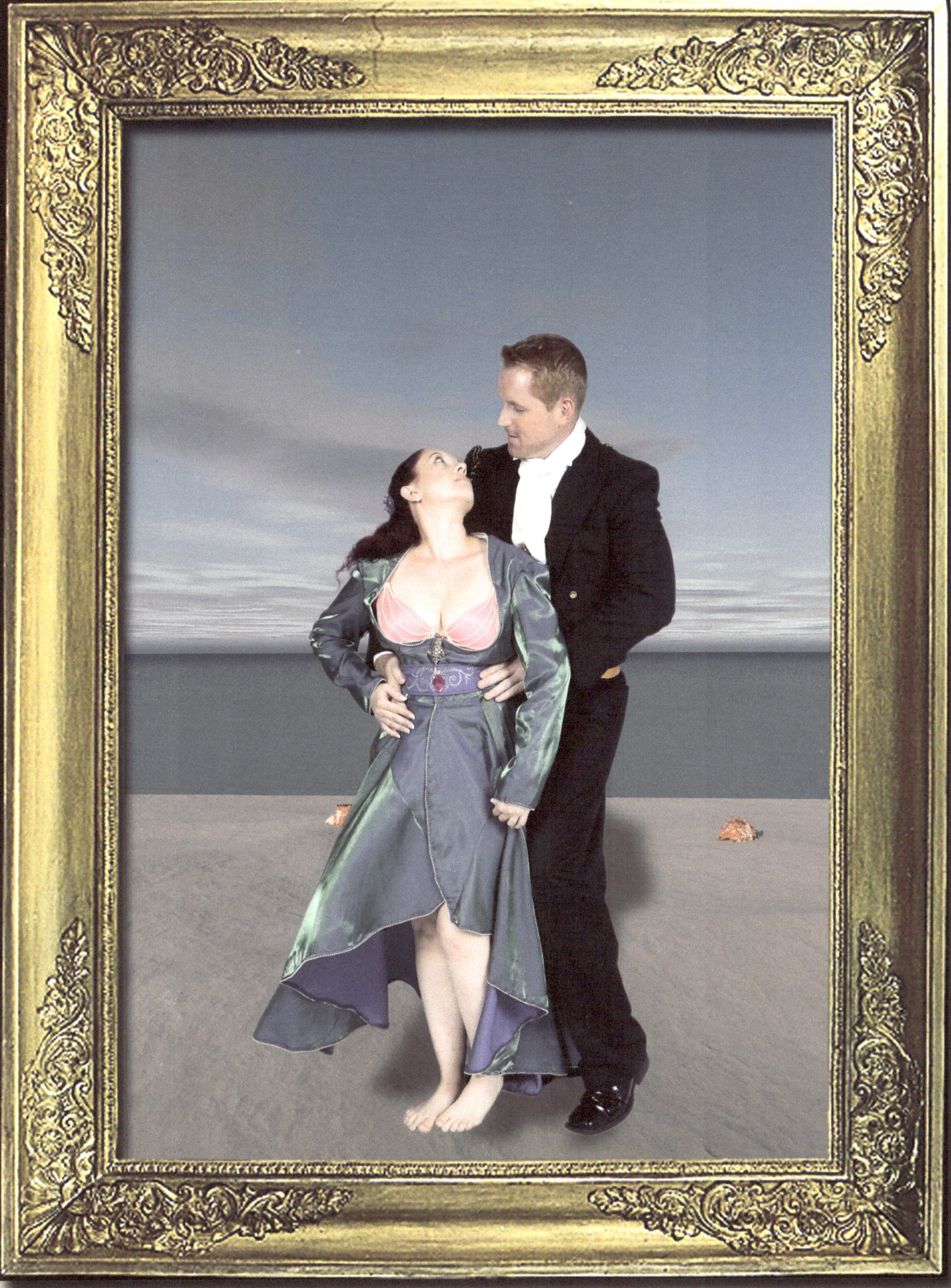

He set her free

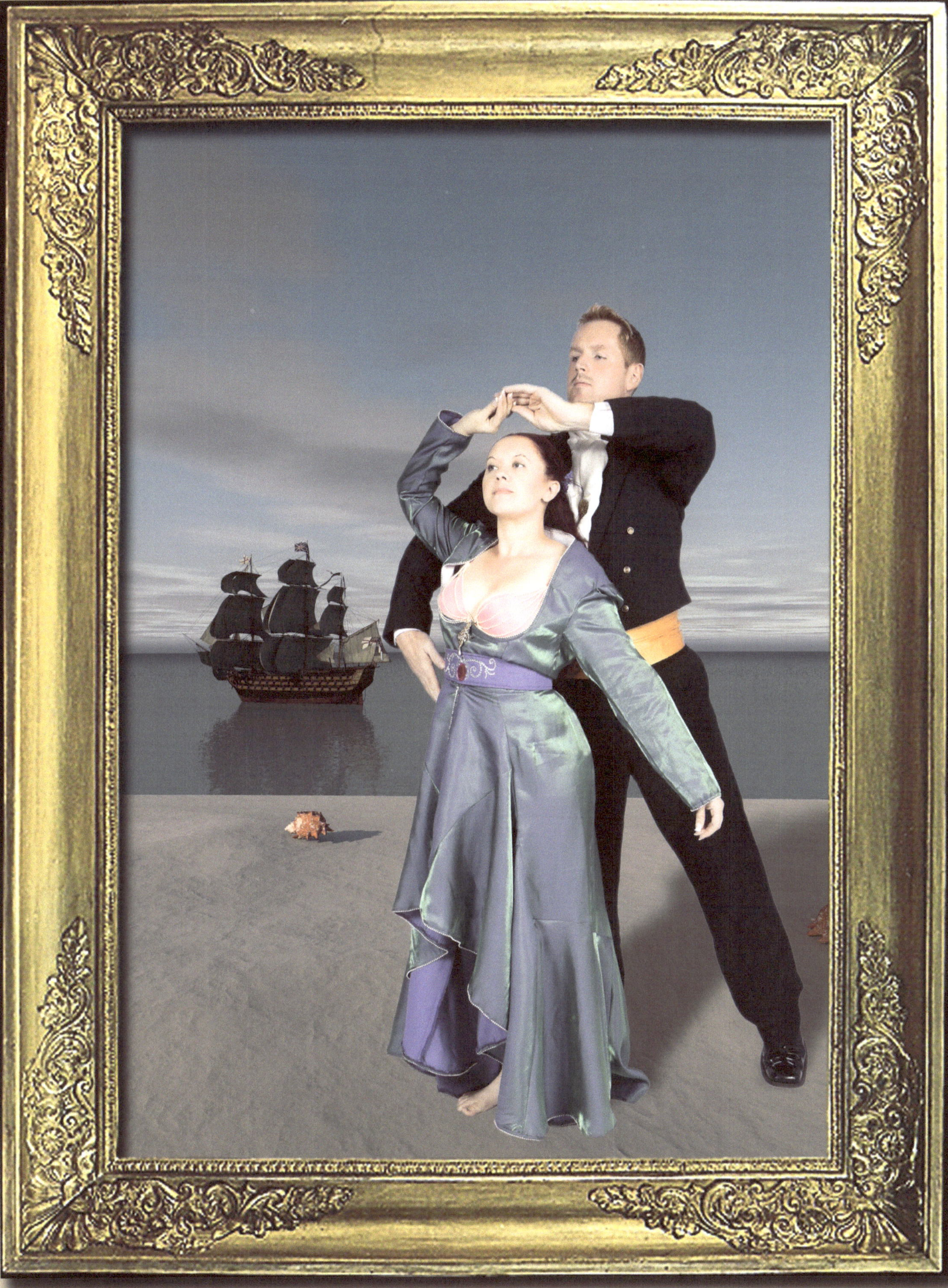

To be her own once more

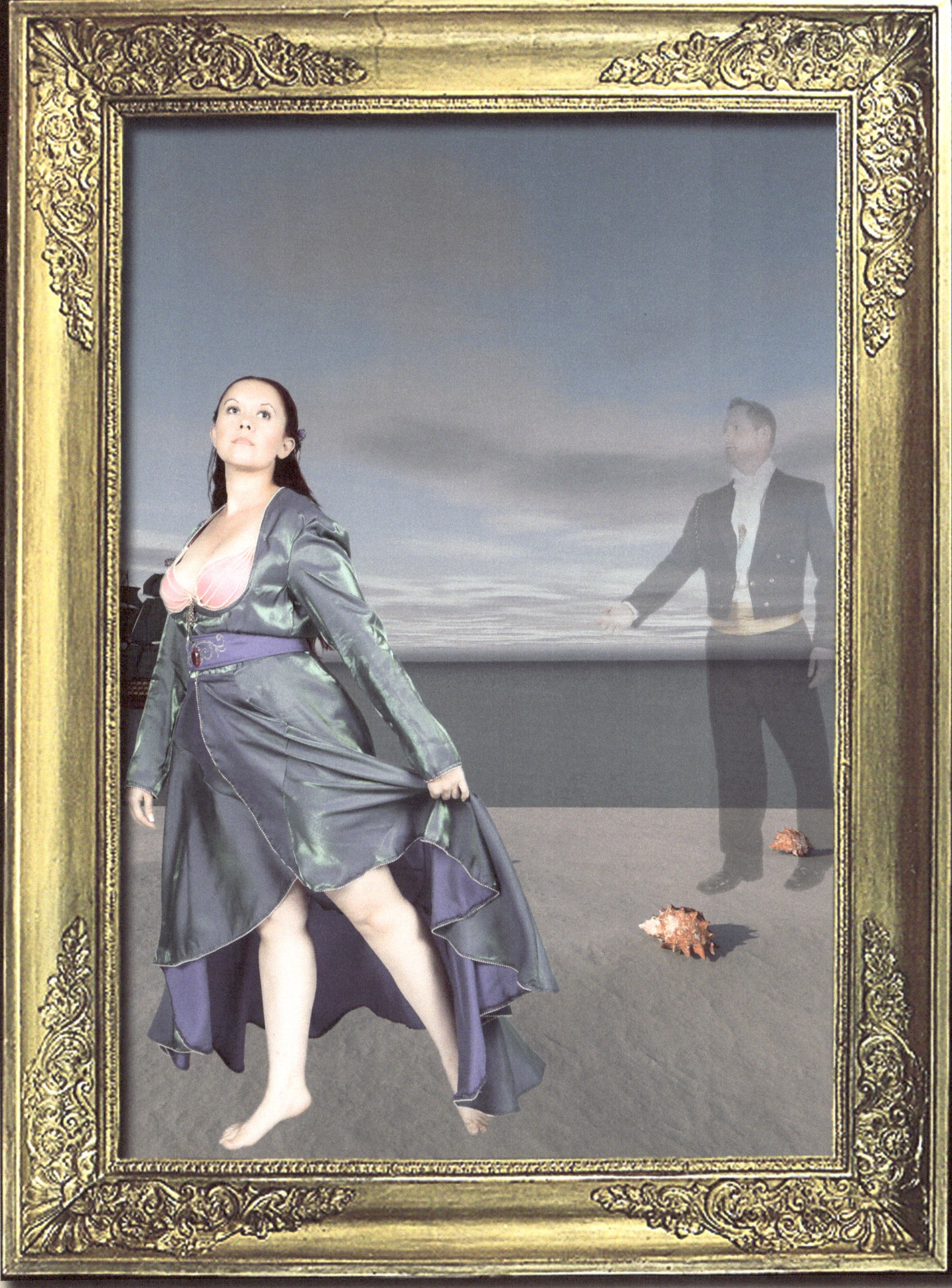

"Until we meet again
my Prince
I'll love you
for all time"

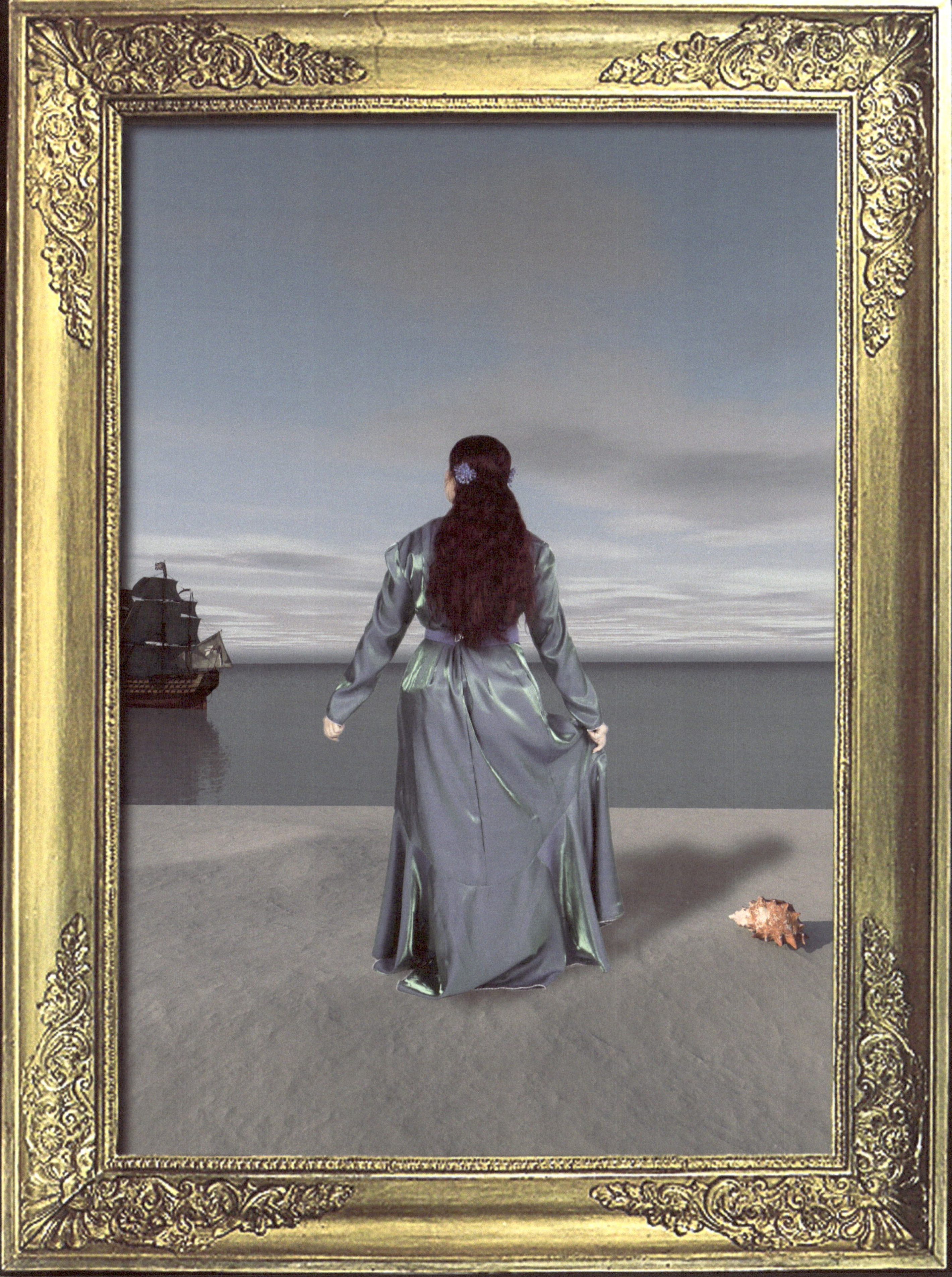

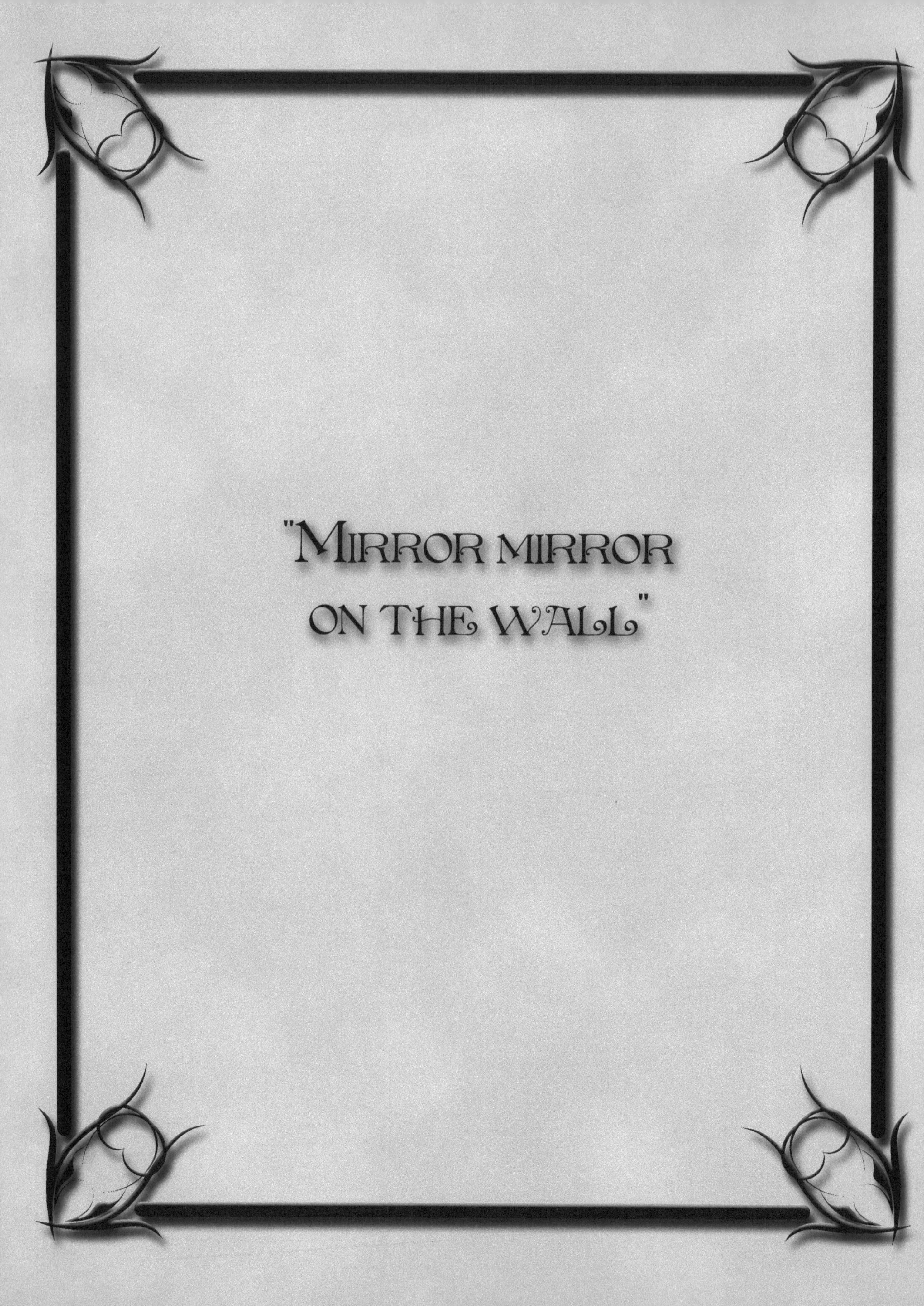
"Mirror mirror
on the wall"

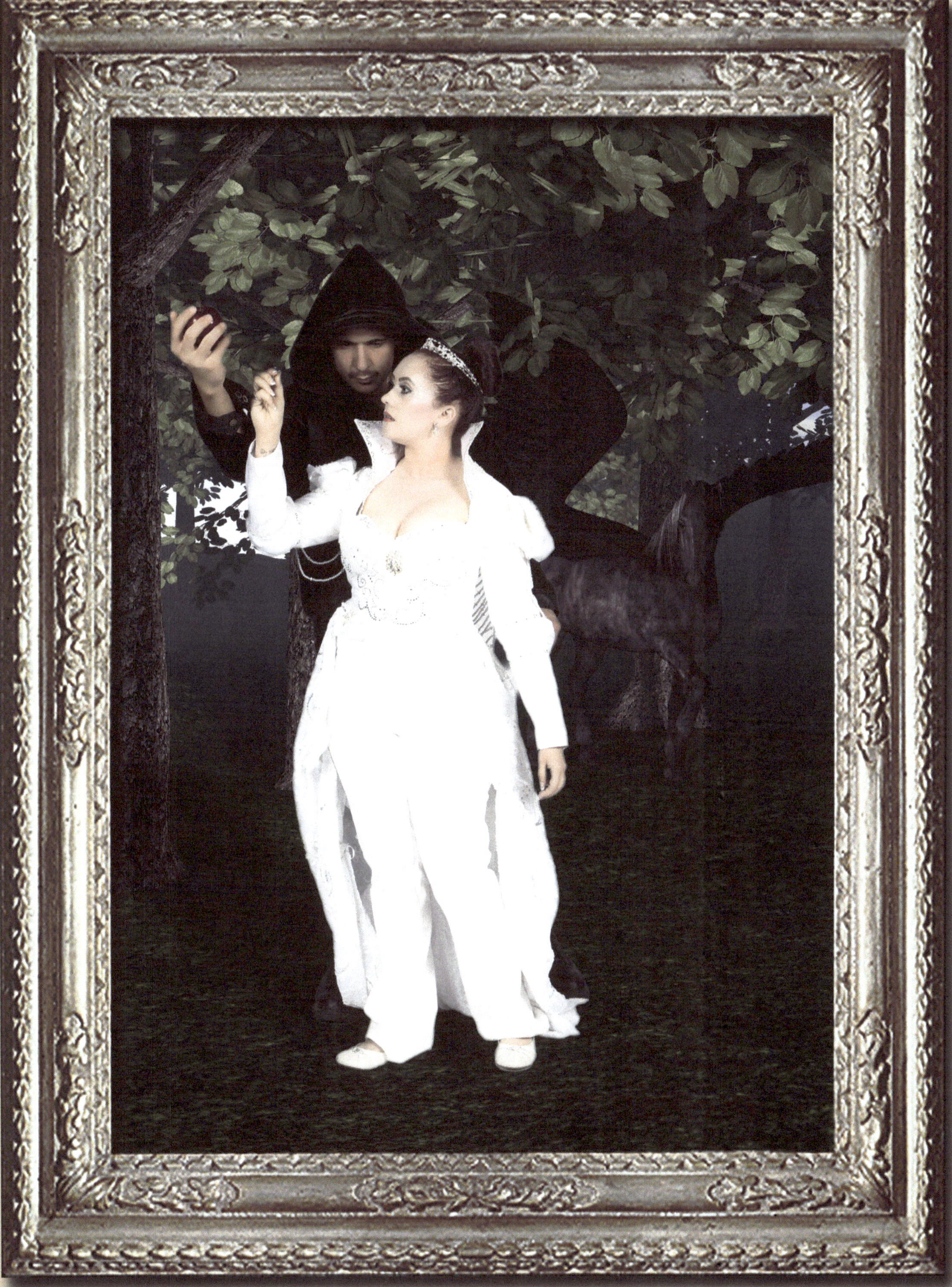

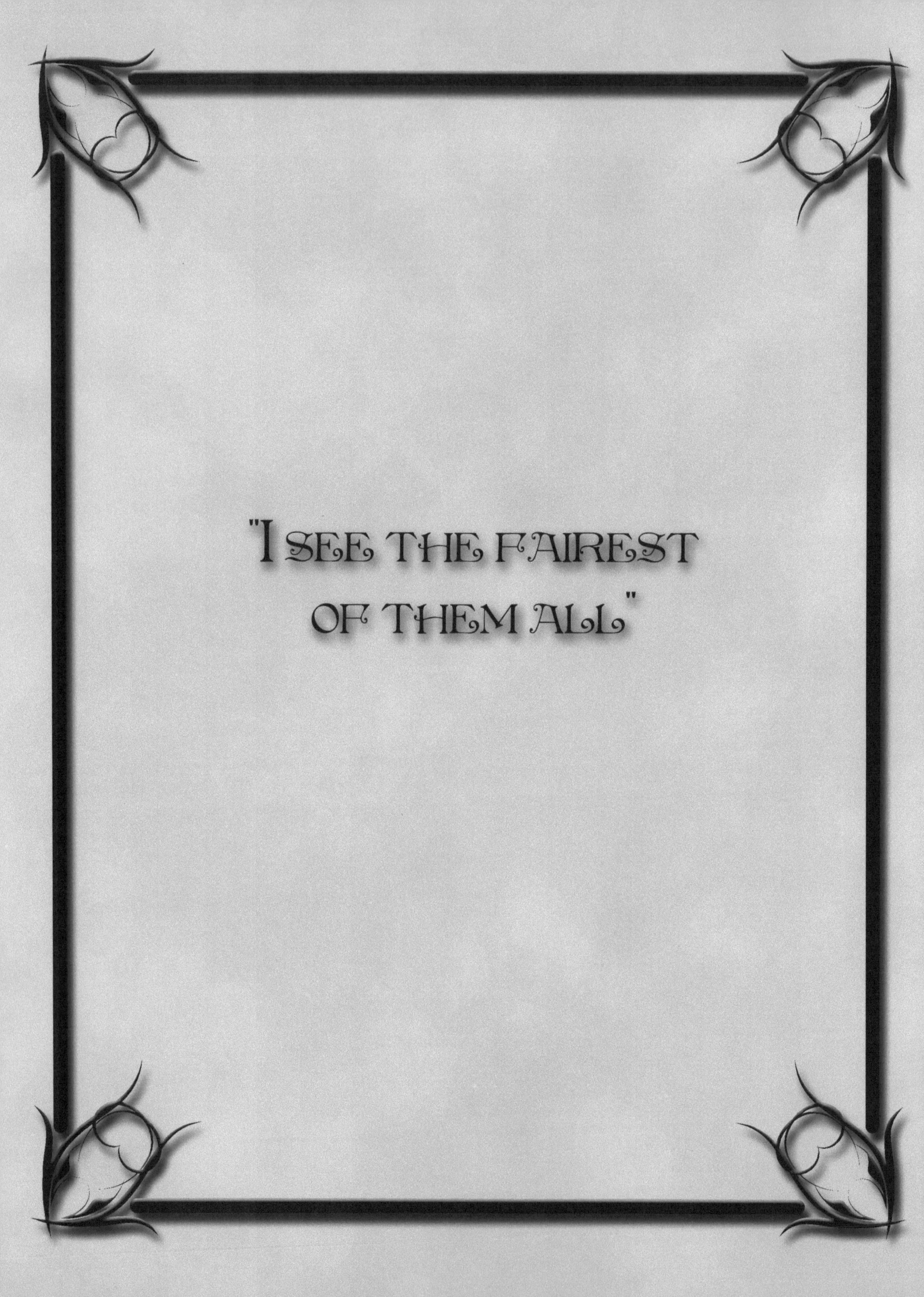
"I SEE THE FAIREST
OF THEM ALL"

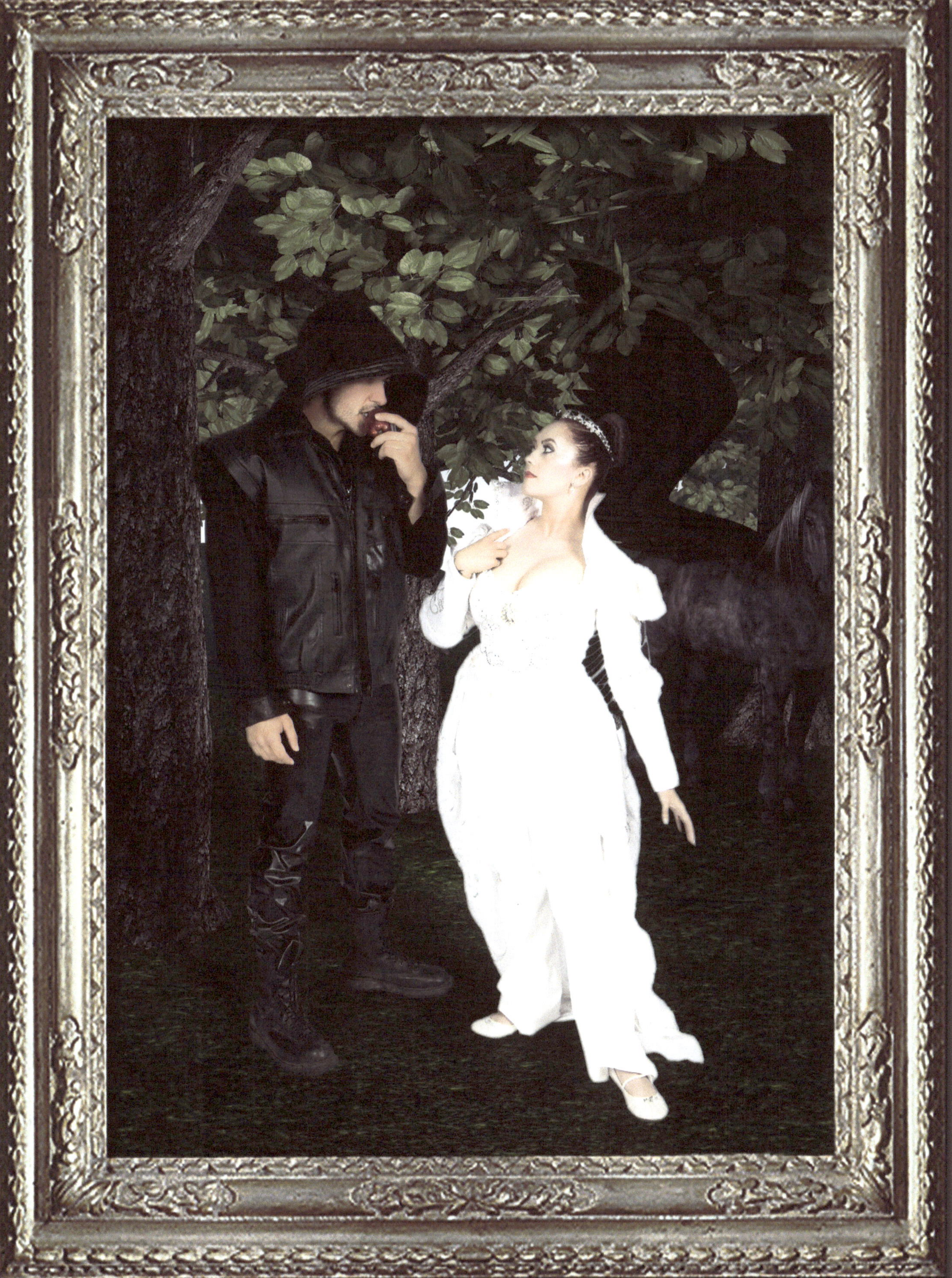

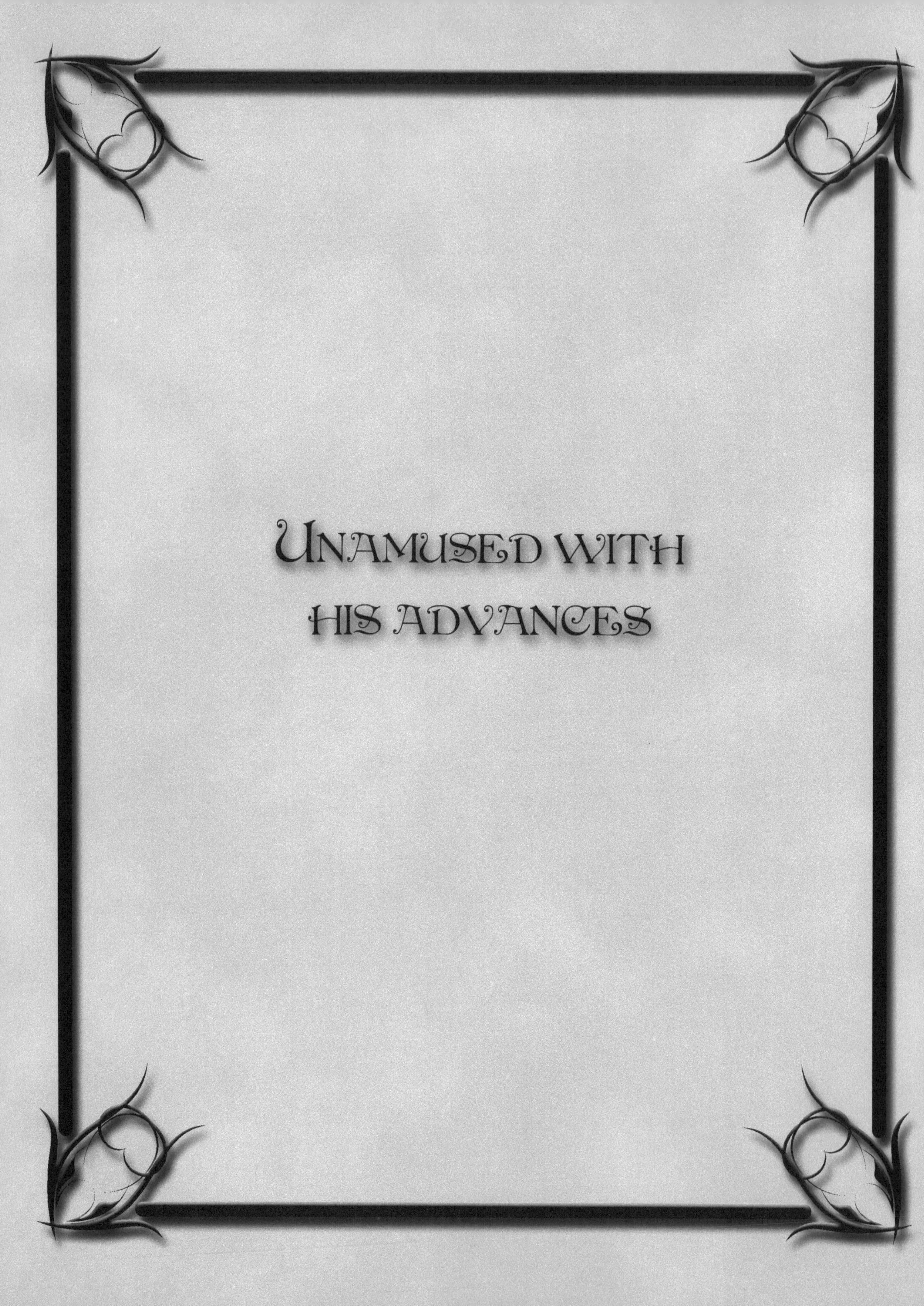

Unamused with his advances

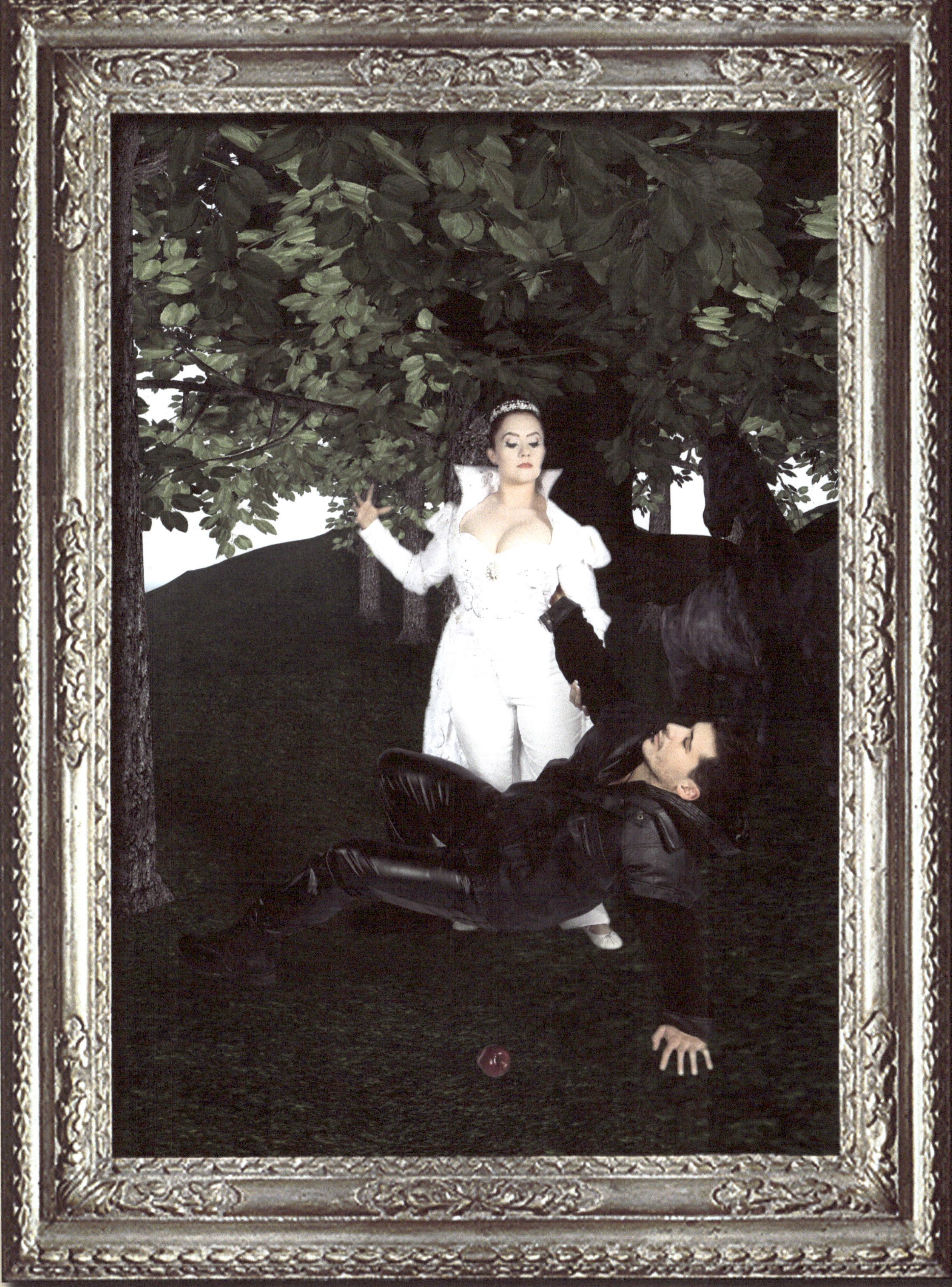

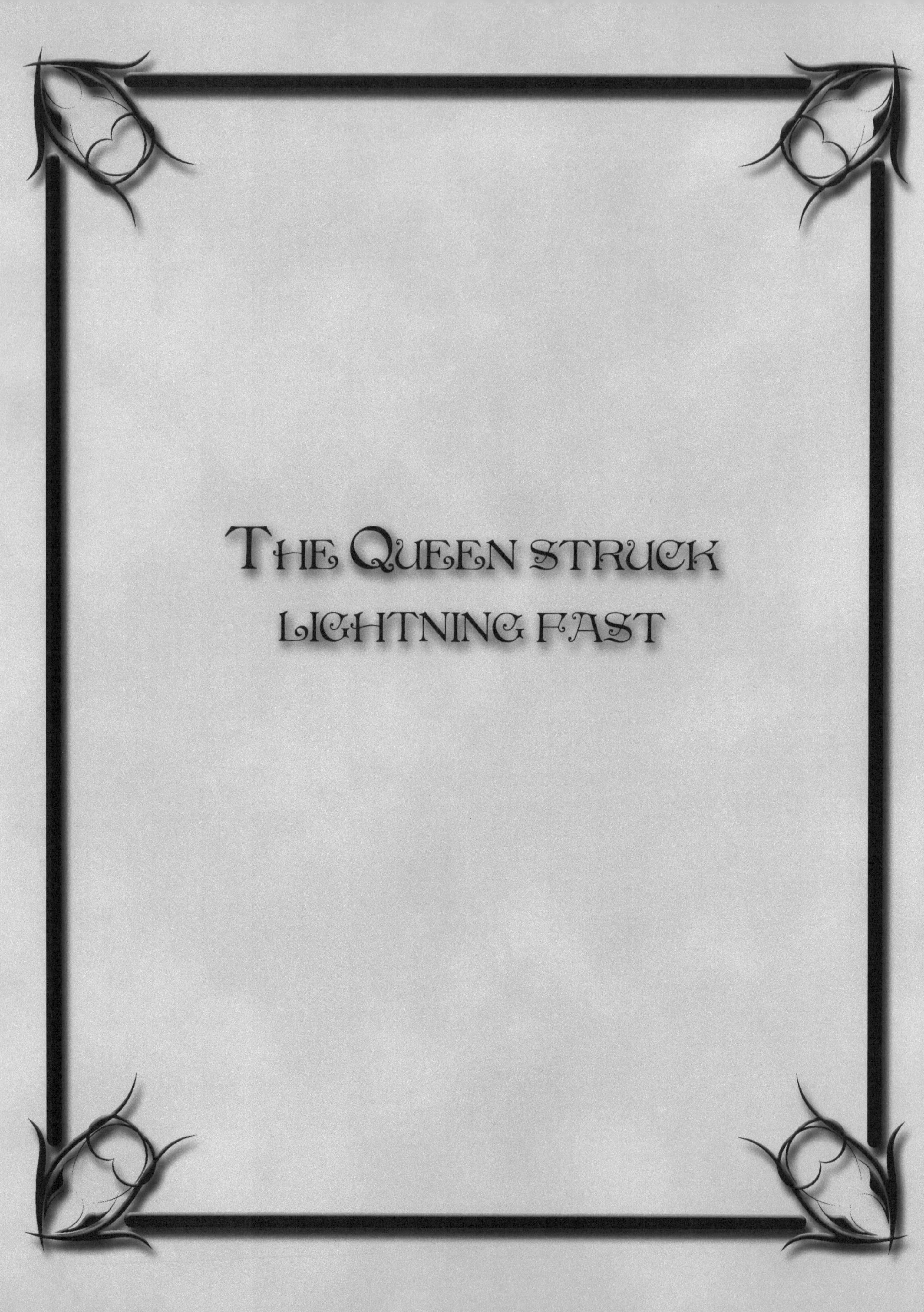

THE QUEEN STRUCK LIGHTNING FAST

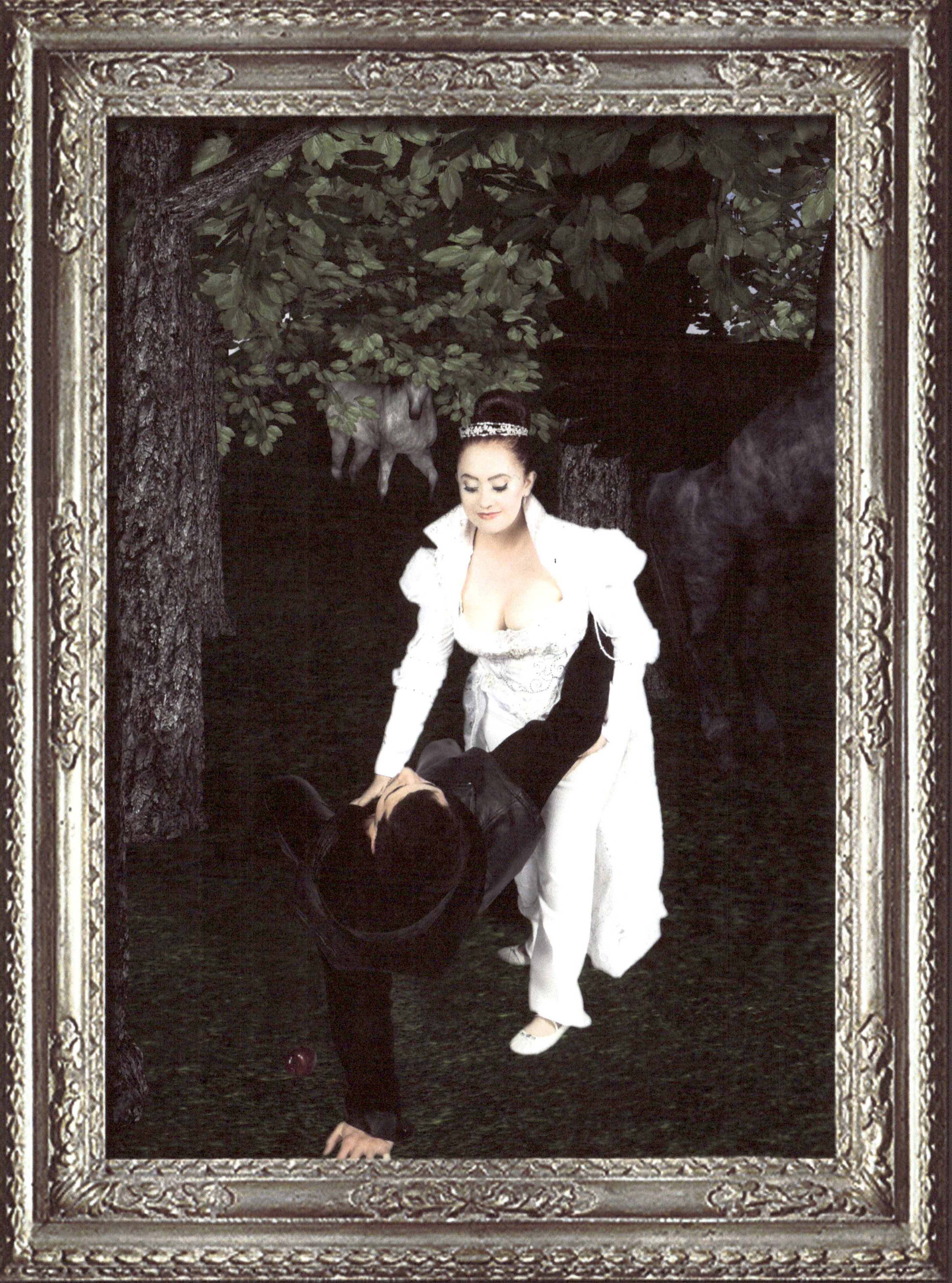

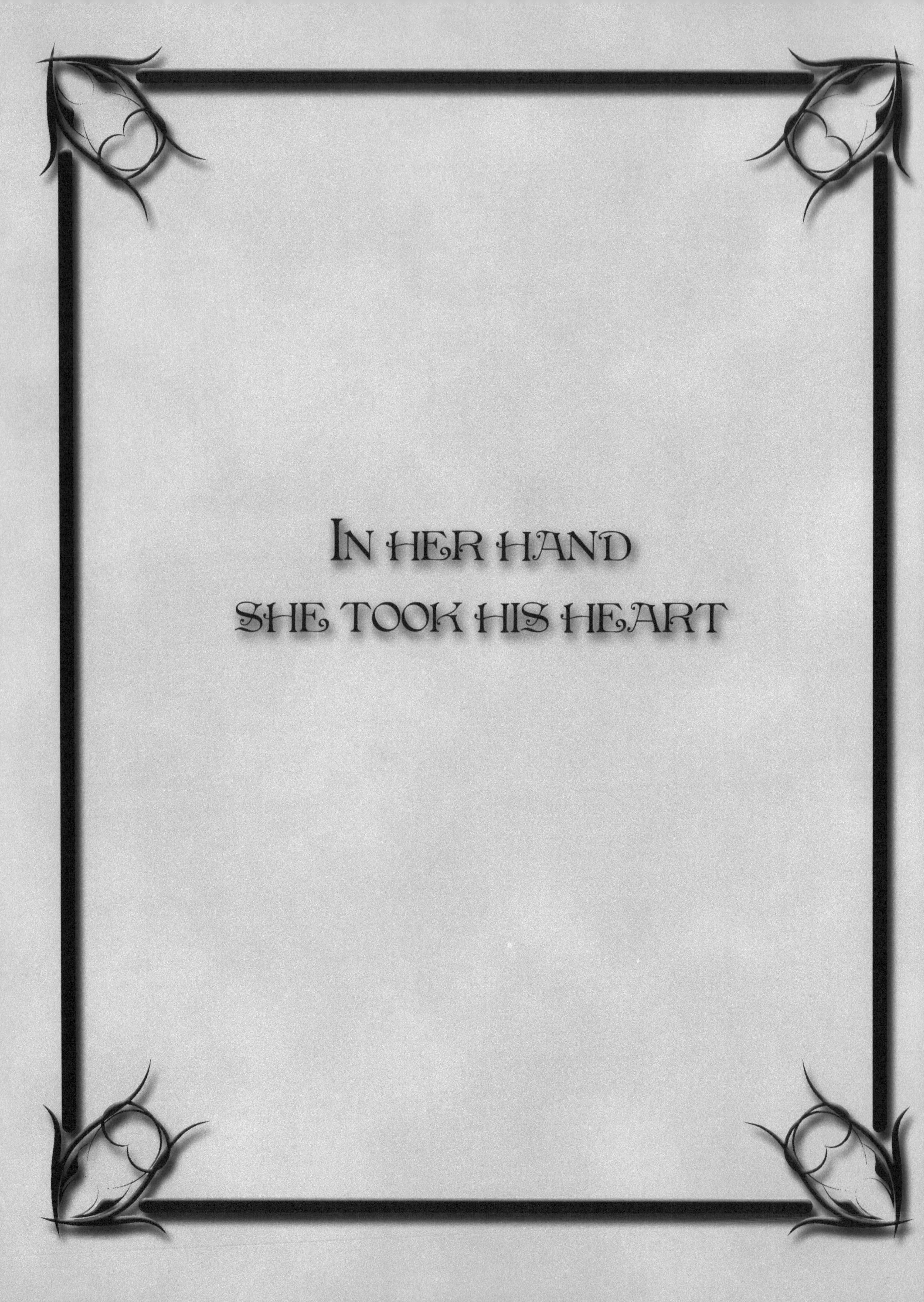
In her hand
she took his heart

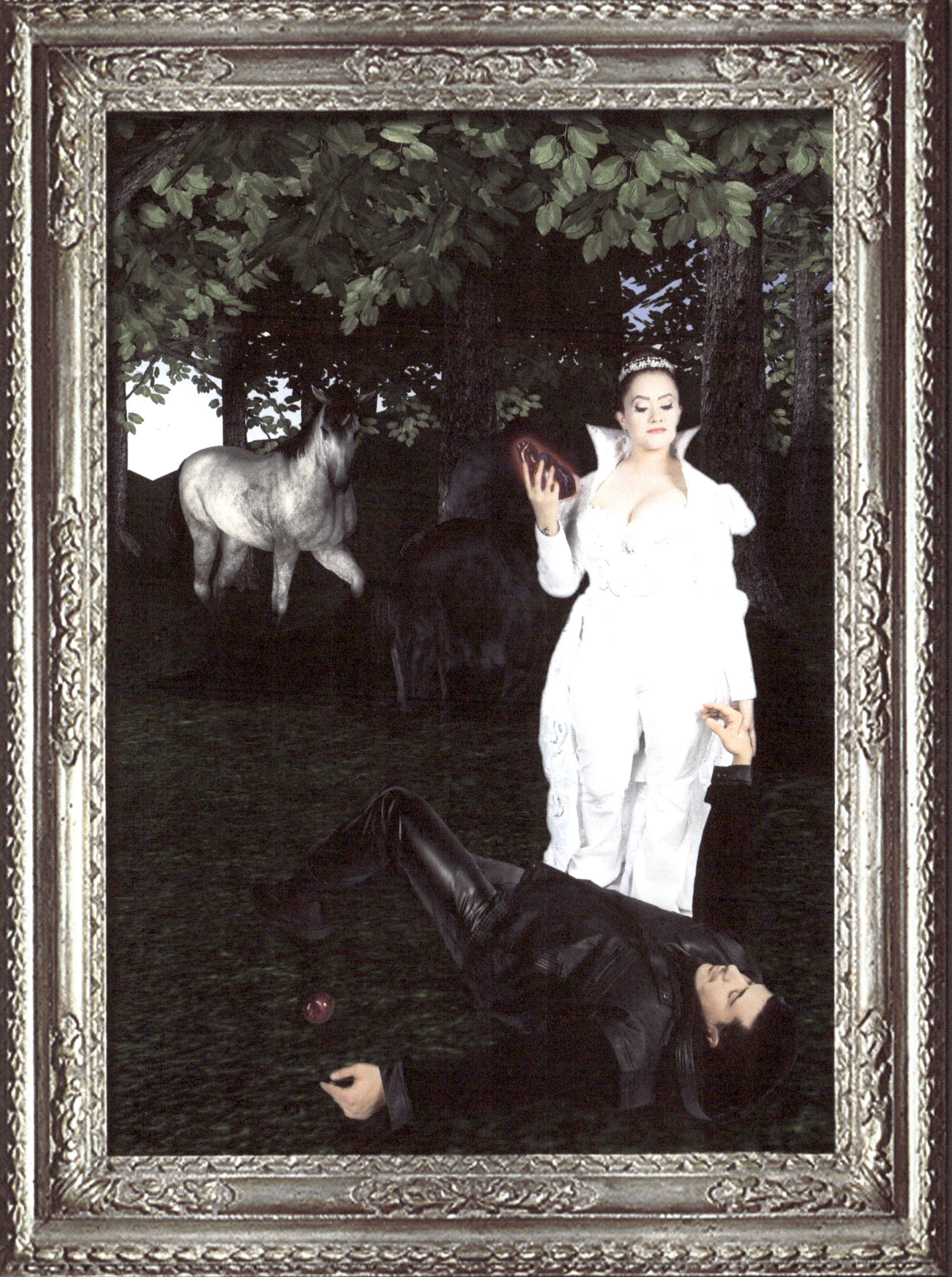

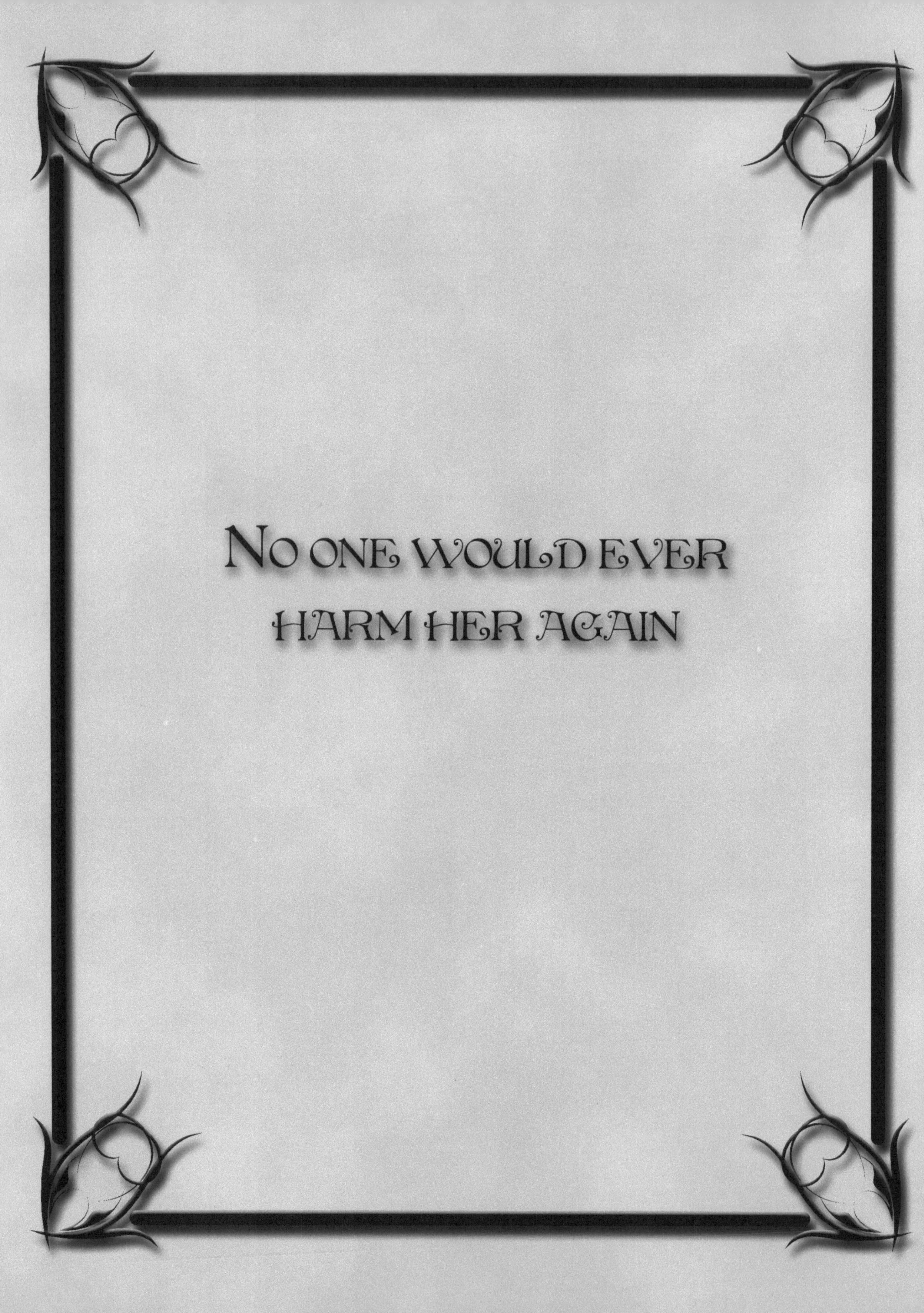

No one would ever harm her again

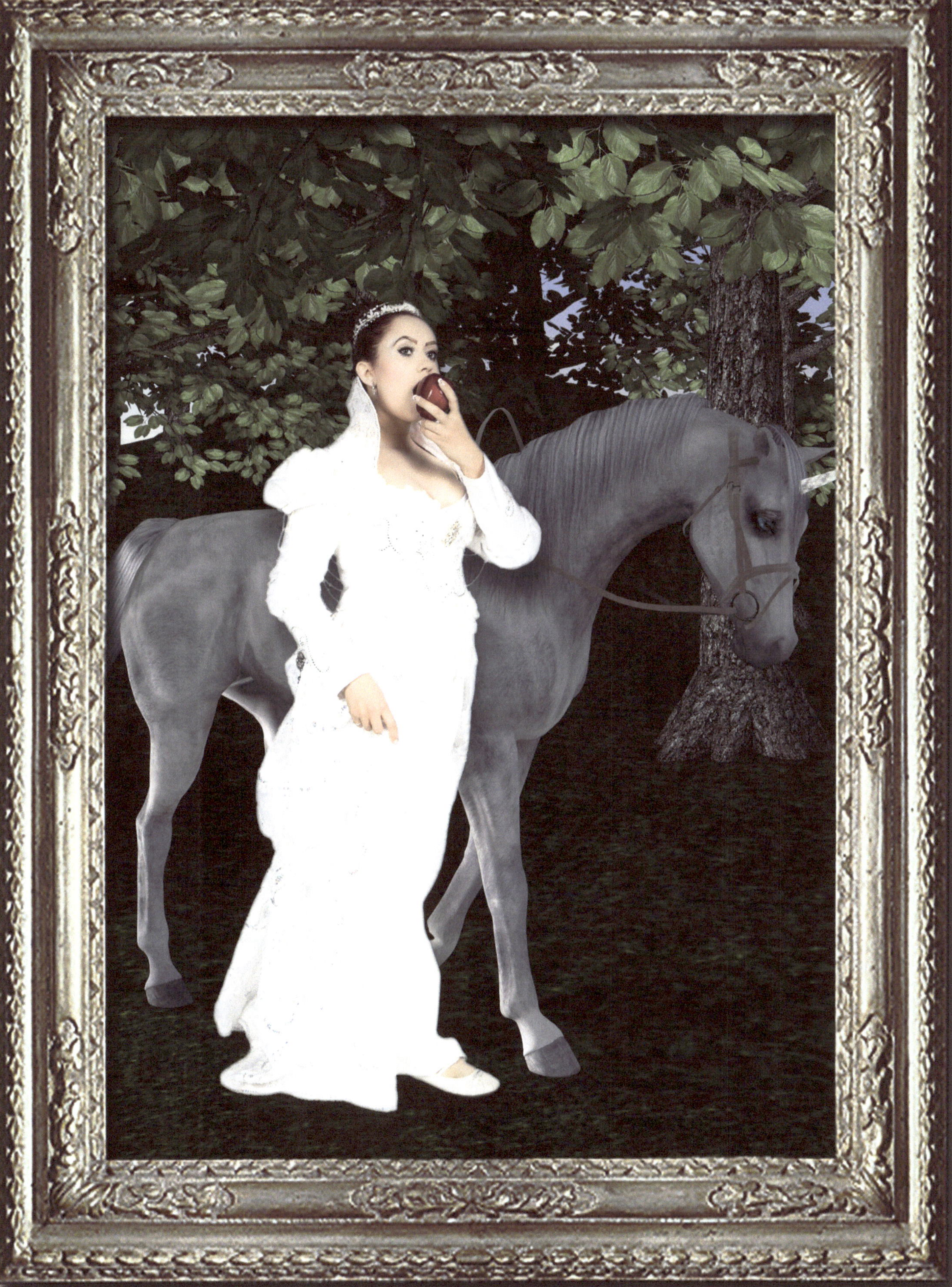

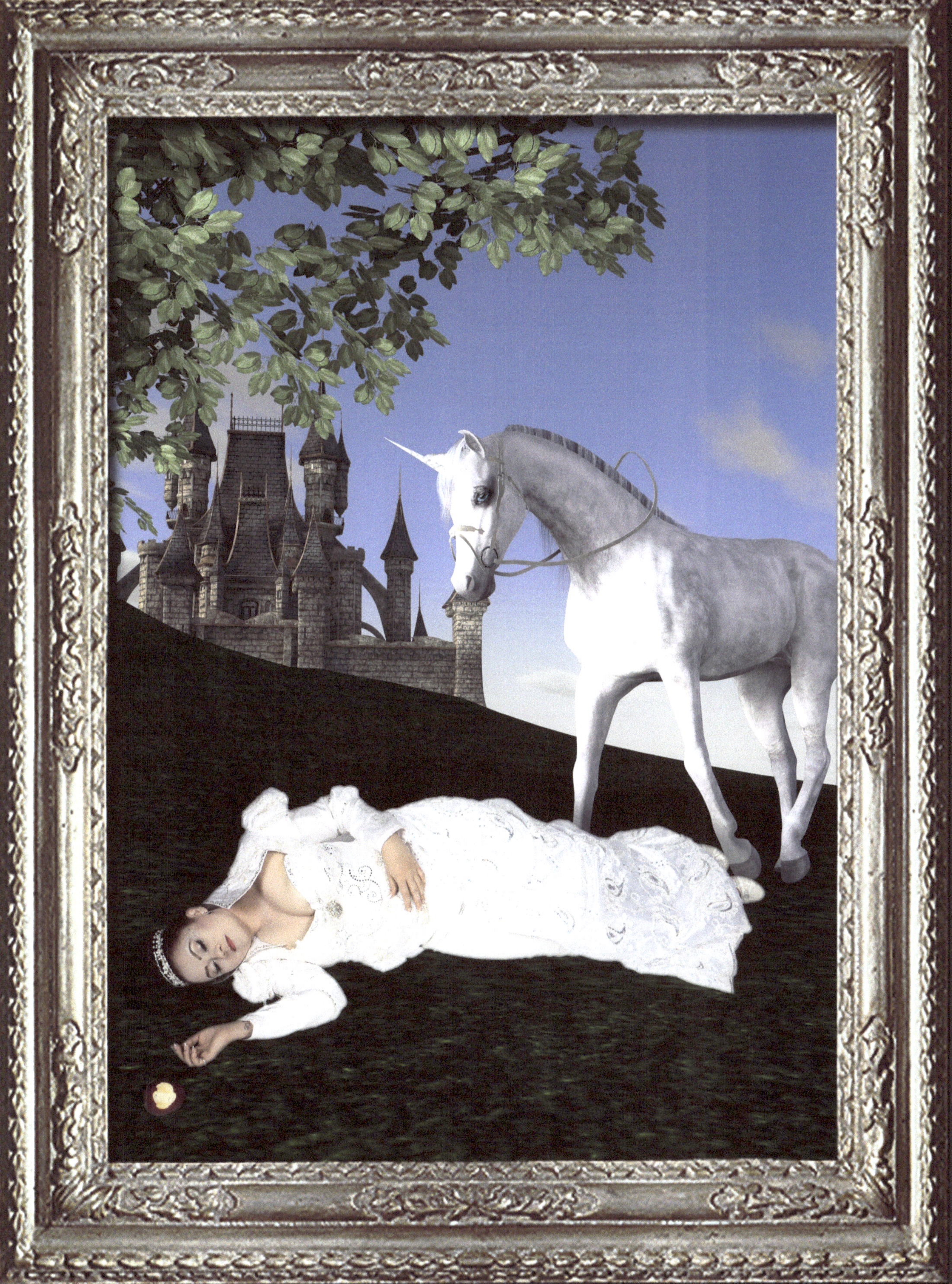

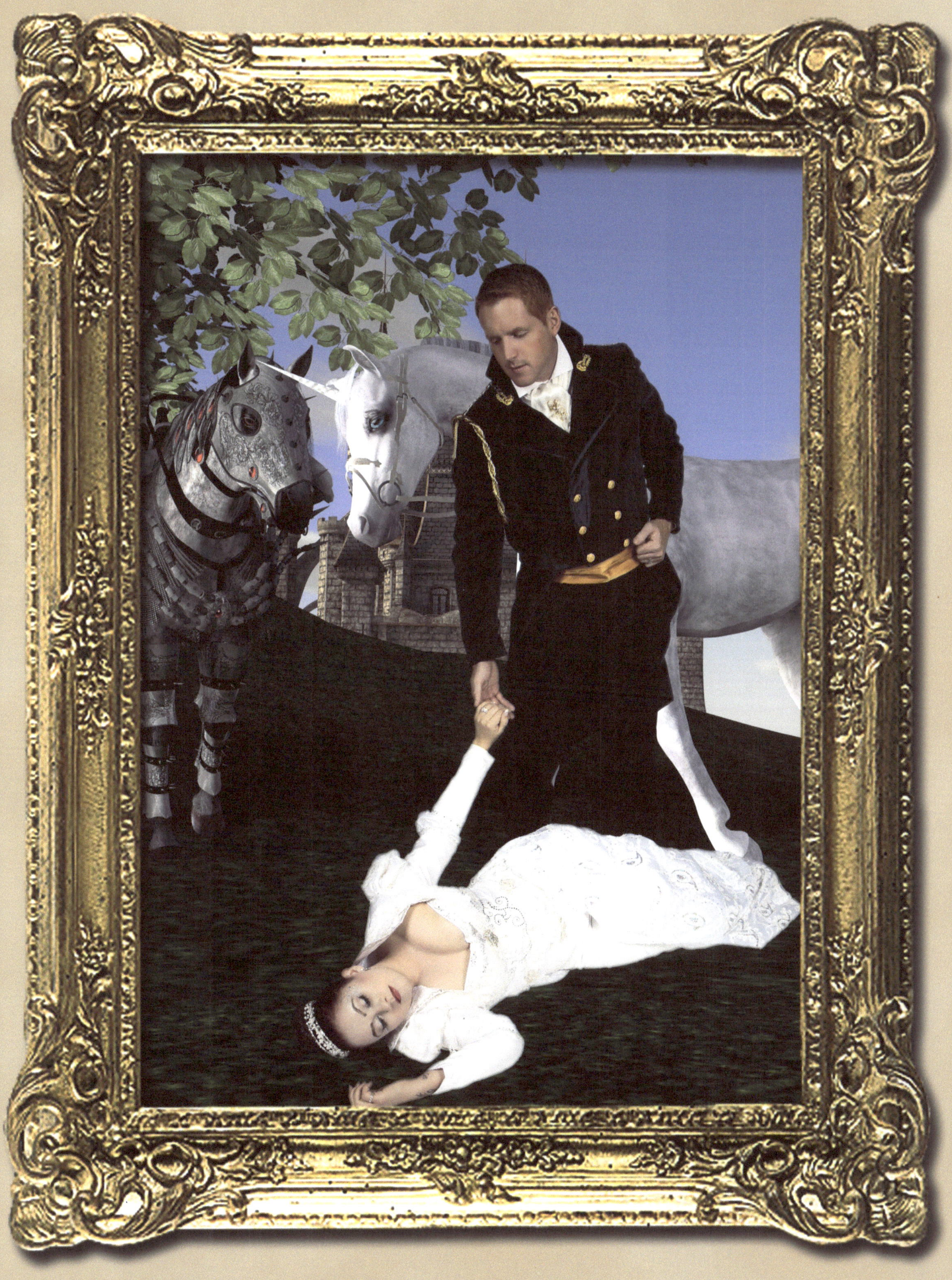

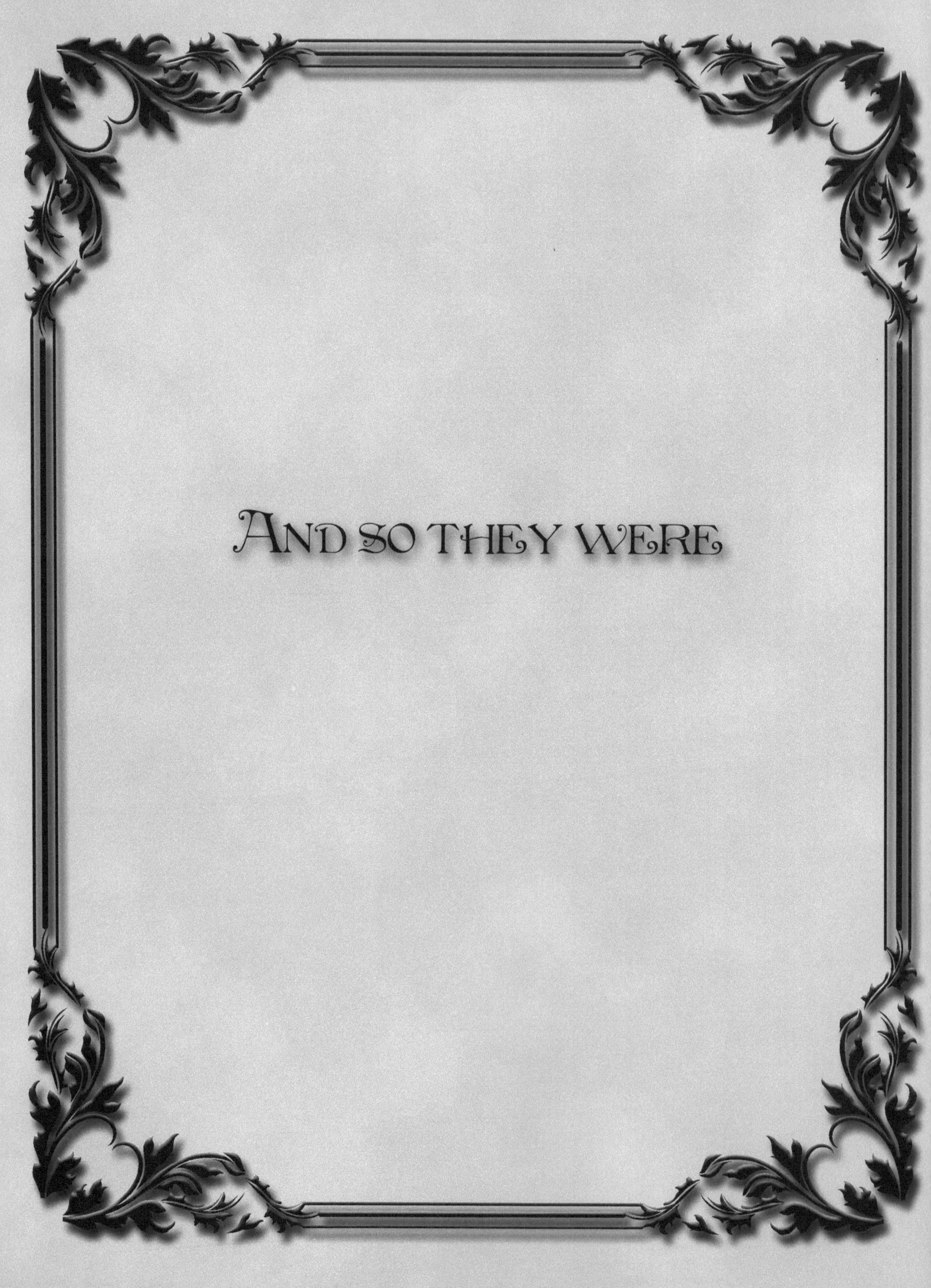

AND SO THEY WERE

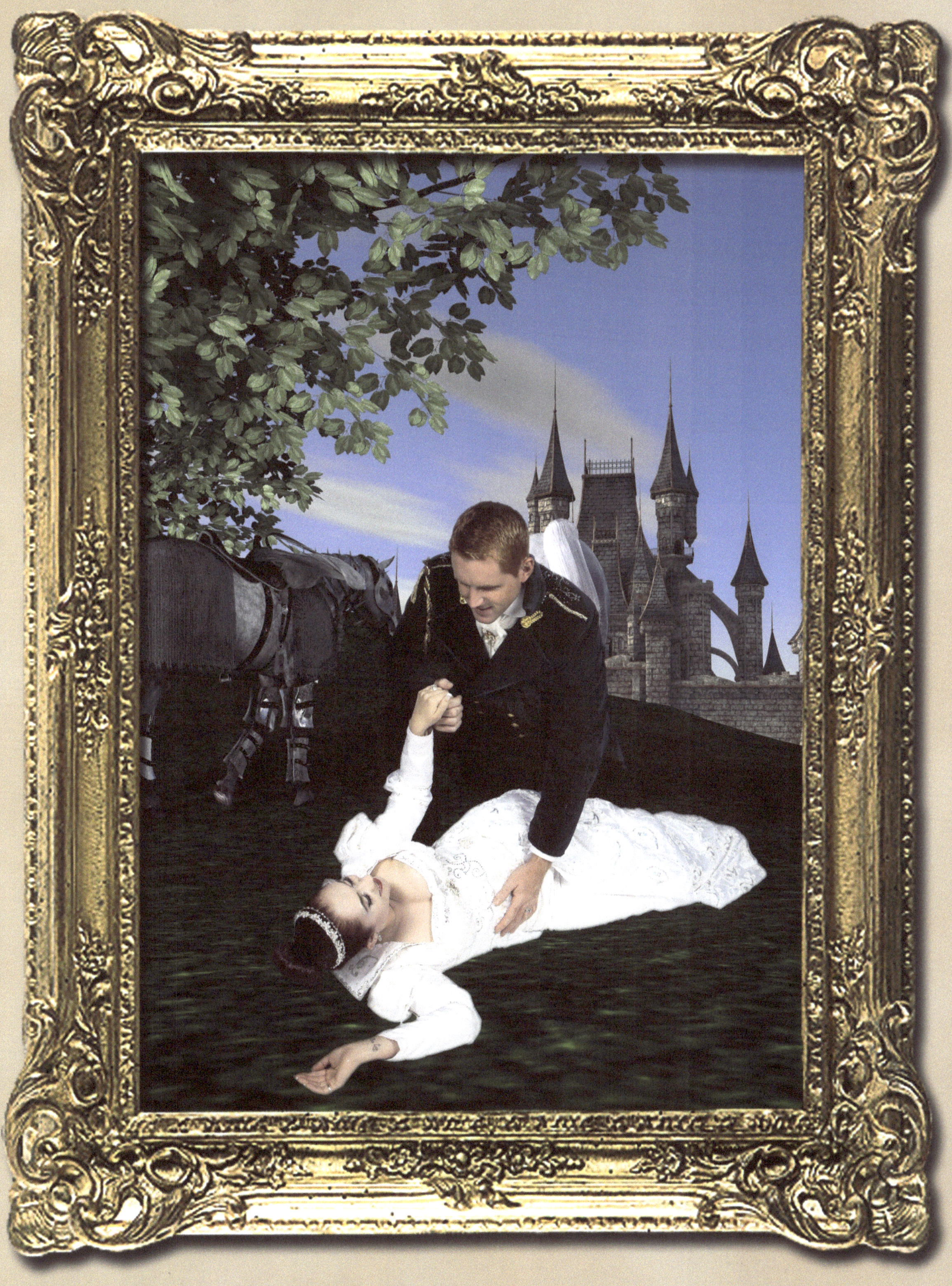

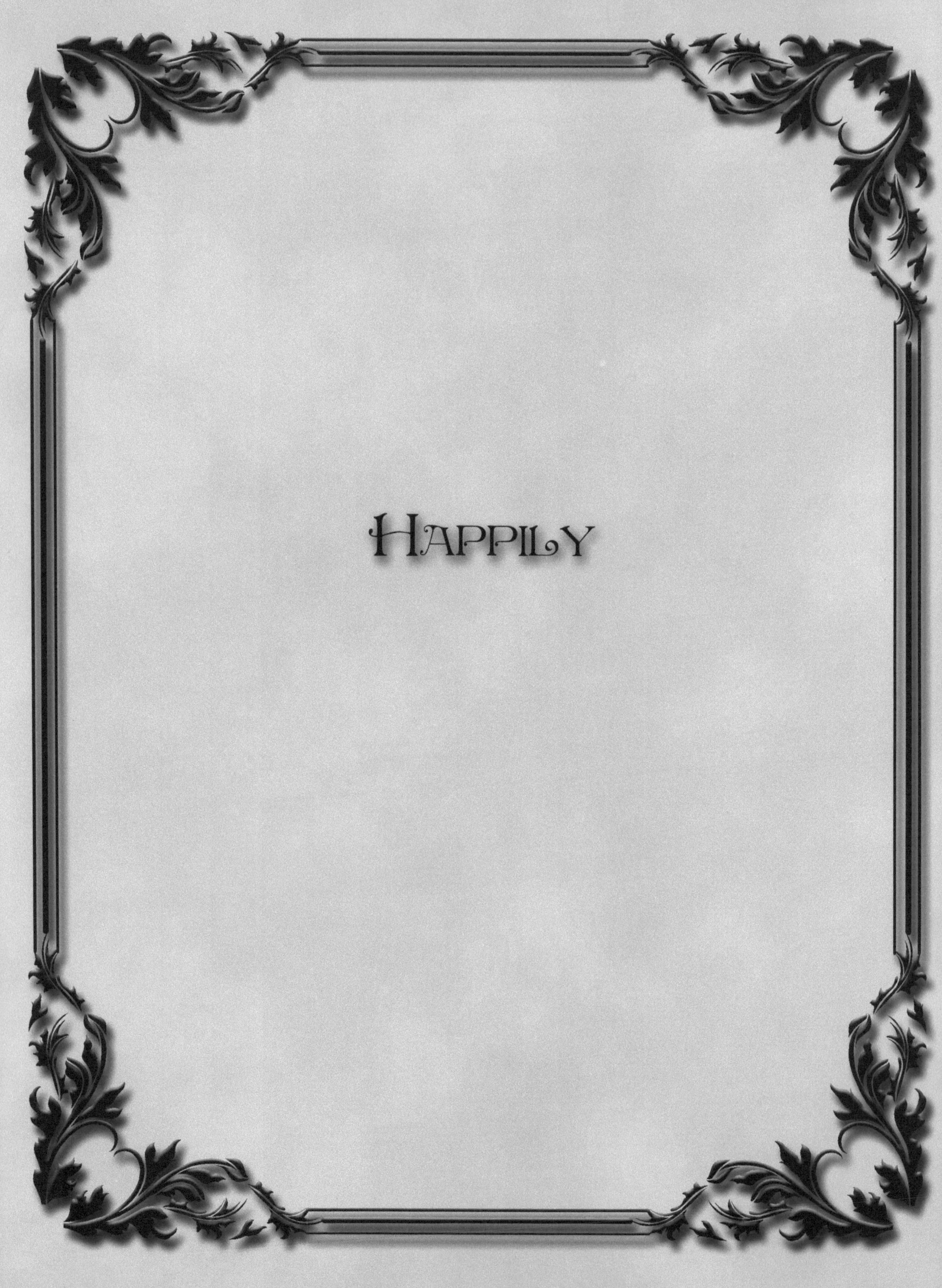
HAPPILY

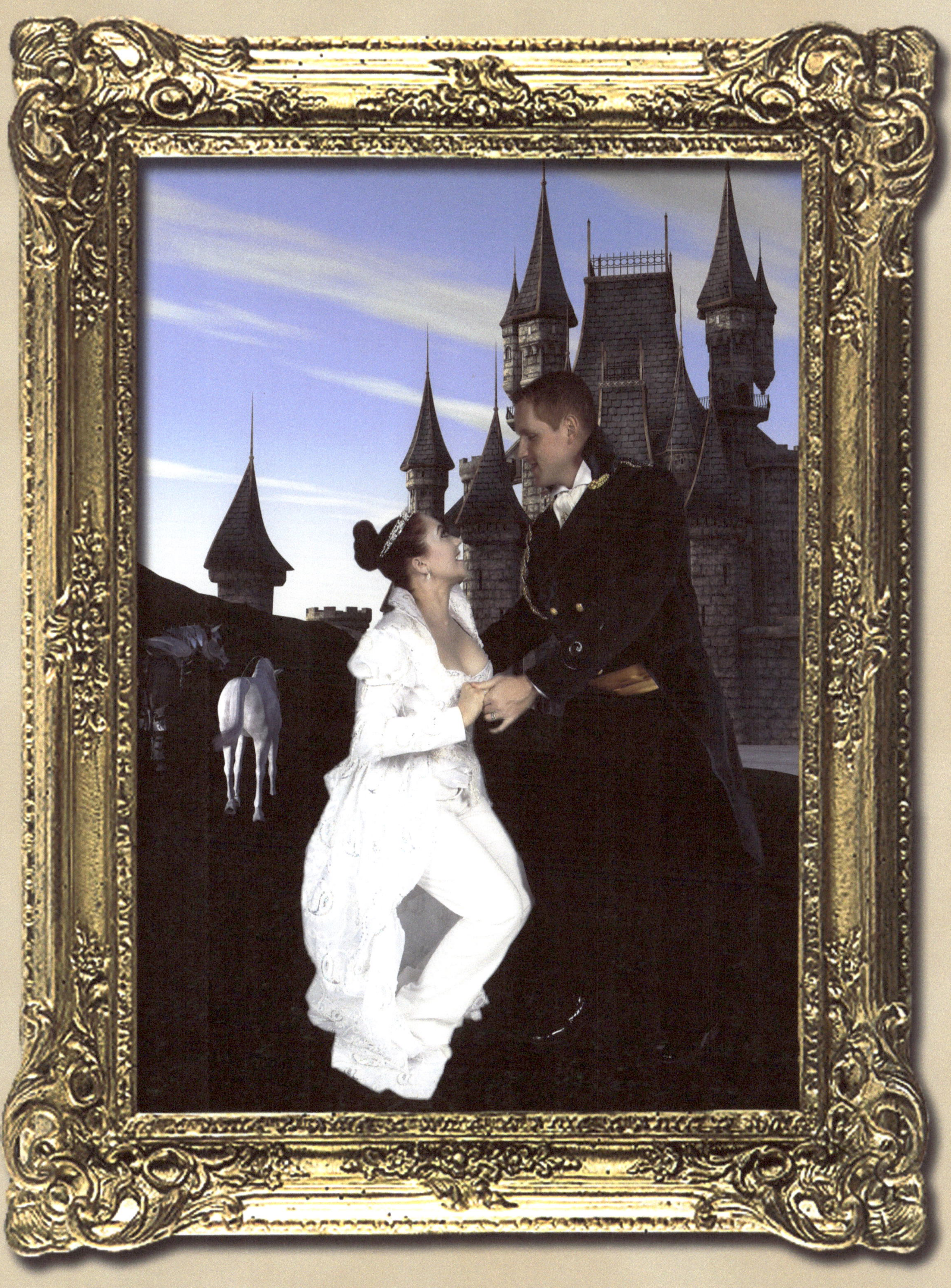

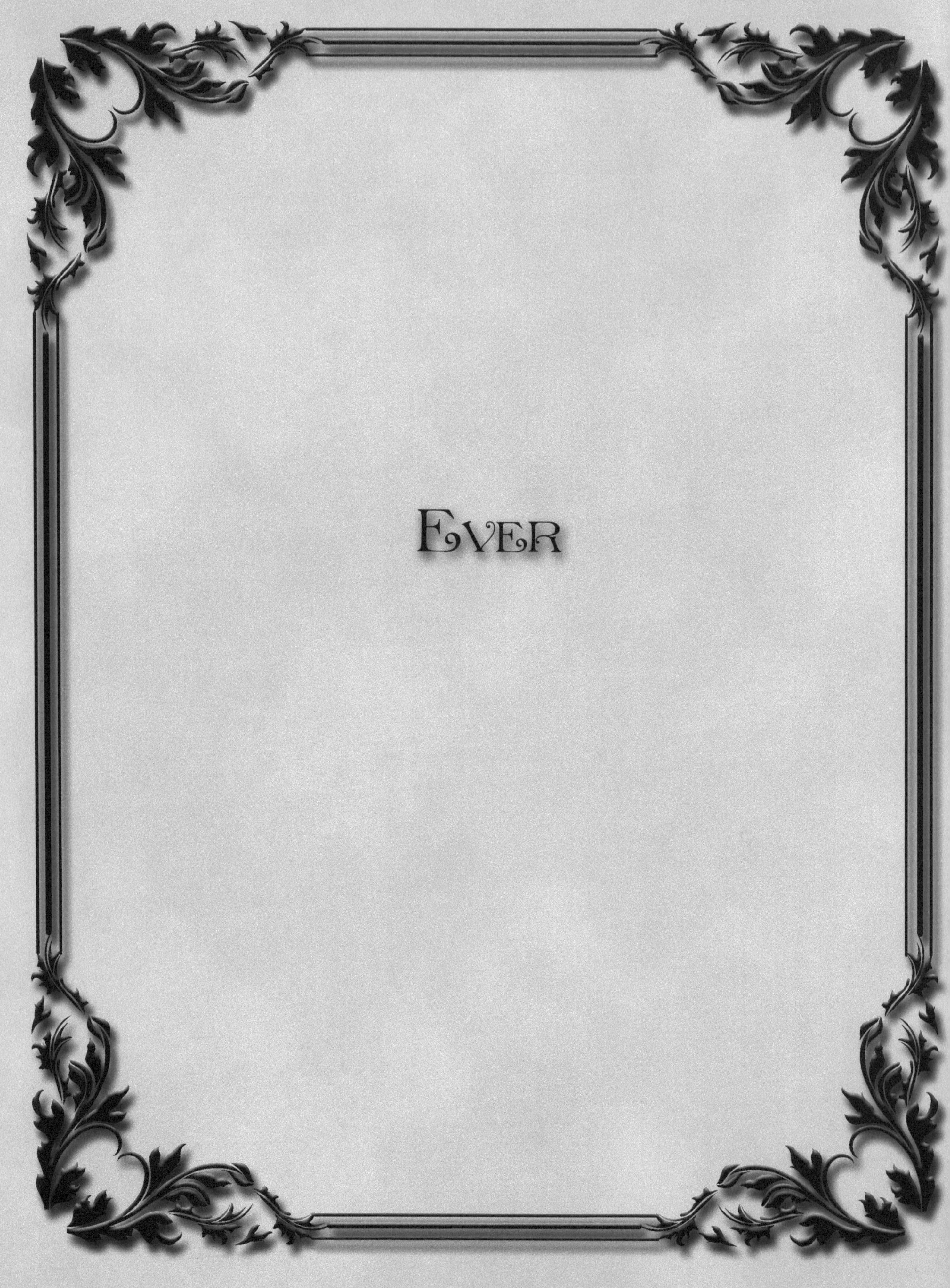

Ever

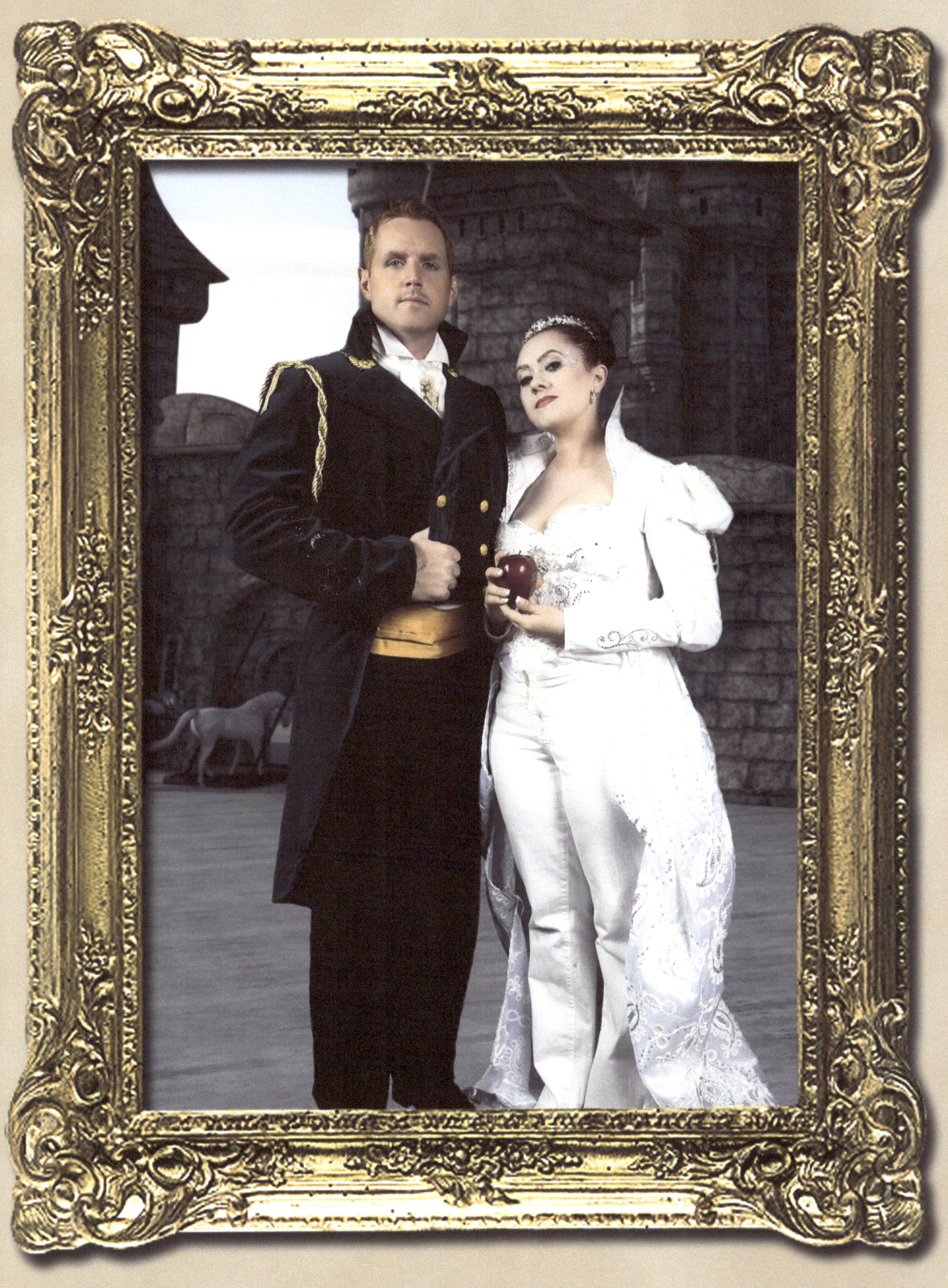

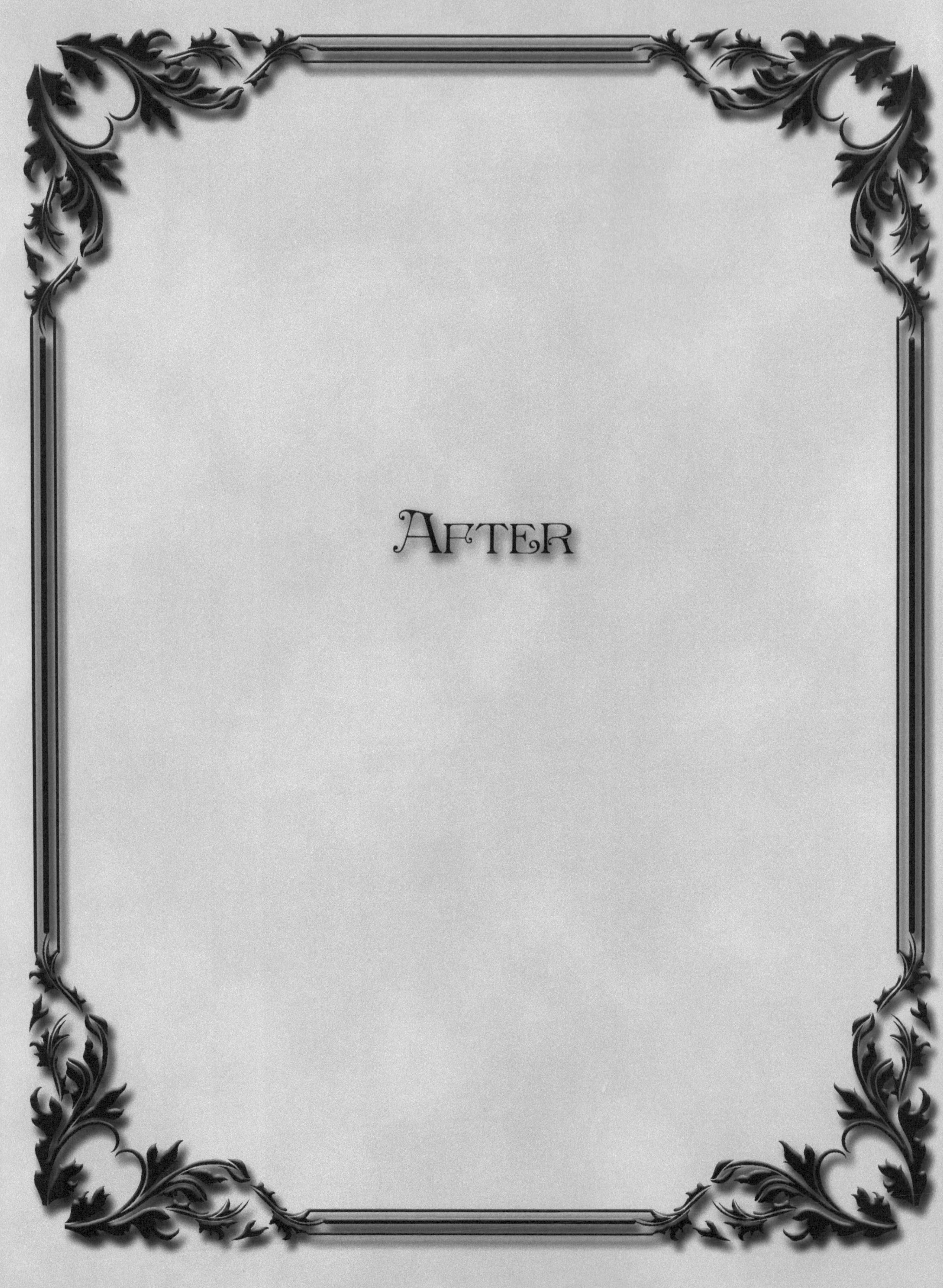

After

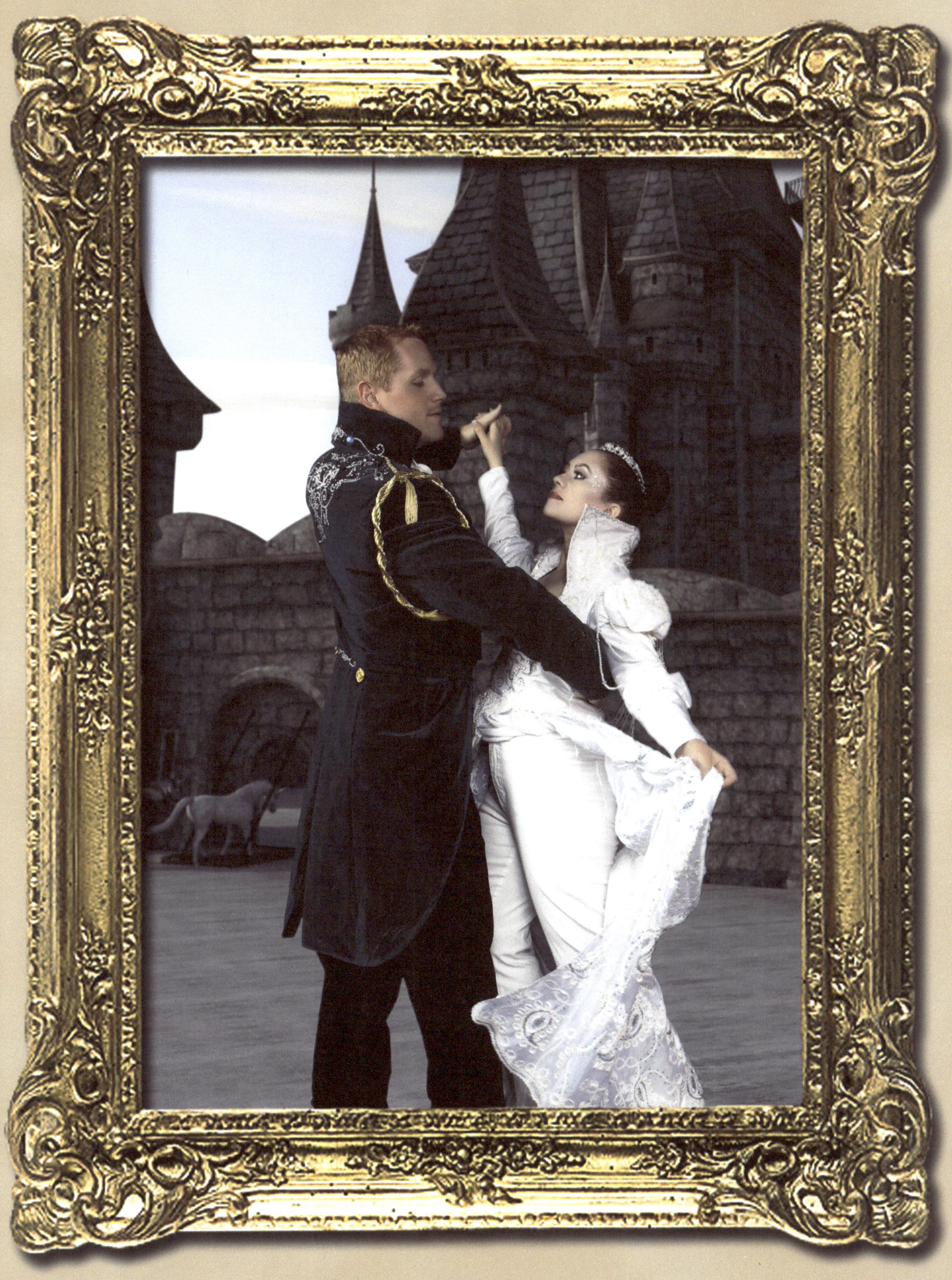

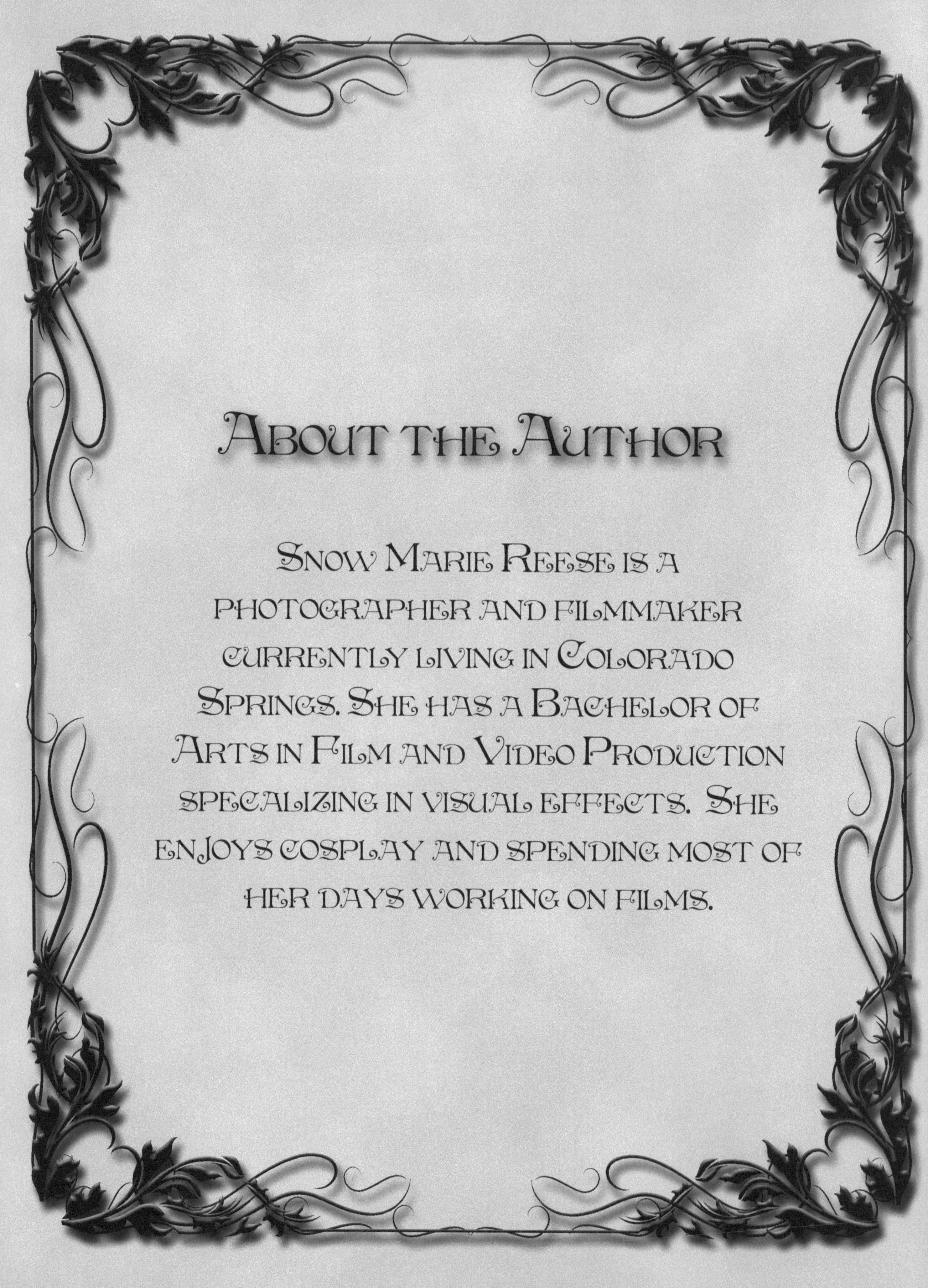

About the Author

Snow Marie Reese is a photographer and filmmaker currently living in Colorado Springs. She has a Bachelor of Arts in Film and Video Production specalizing in visual effects. She enjoys cosplay and spending most of her days working on films.

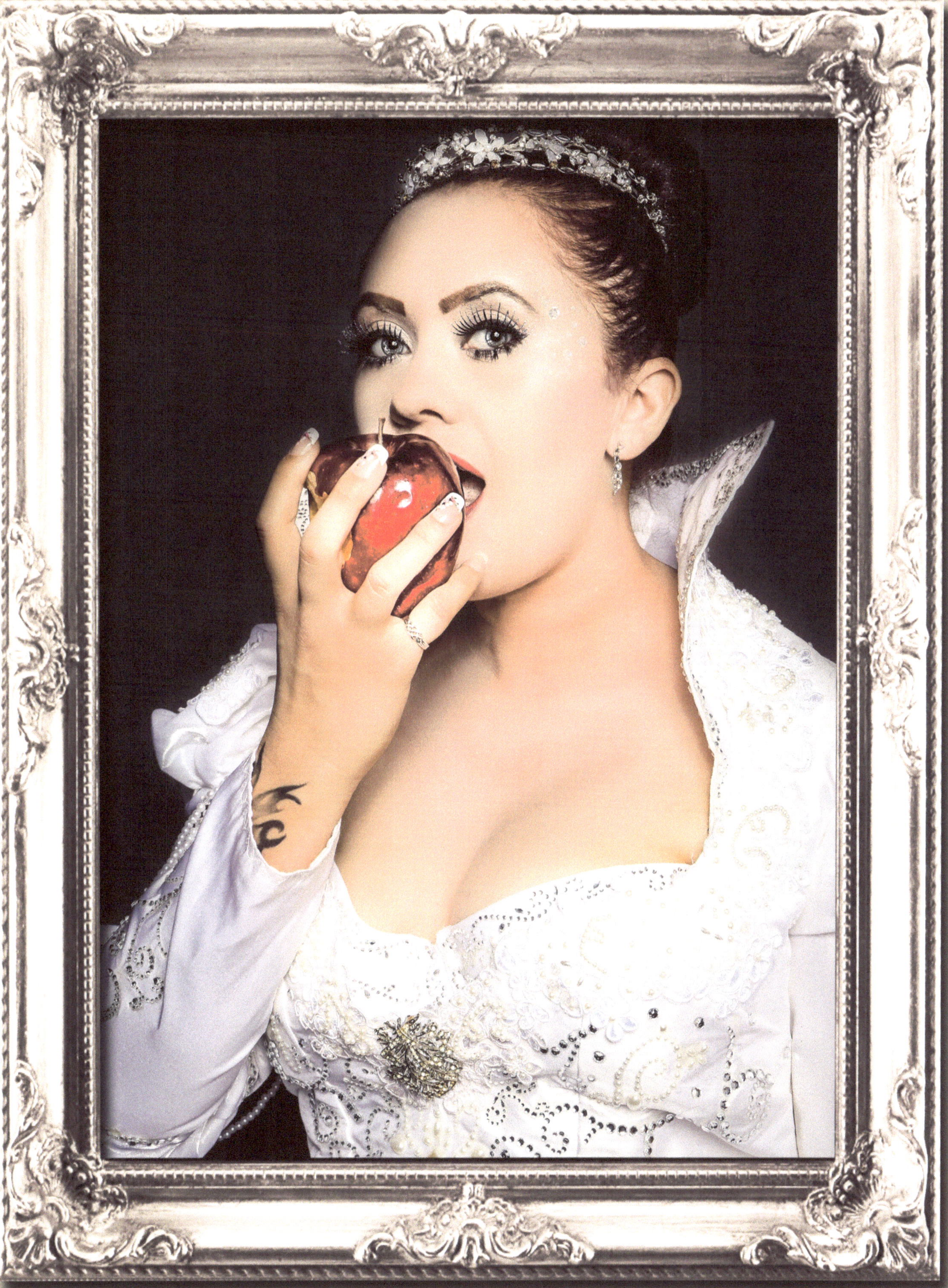

www.ingramcontent.com/pod-product-compliance
Lightning Source LLC
LaVergne TN
LVHW070508120826
845147LV00031BA/259

* 9 7 8 0 9 8 6 2 3 5 8 2 5 *